THE TEXA[...]

All the news tha[...]

Fortune Neme[...]

Clint Lockhart, sentenced to life imprisonment for murder, cunningly escaped his shackles last evening while being transferred to a maximum security facility. Guards opened fire on the dangerous jailbird, but he disappeared into the tranquil Texas countryside. Eyewitnesses report that Lockhart may have been wounded by a bullet to the leg. A full-blown manhunt is under way.

A cellmate confessed that just before Lockhart's transfer, the vindictive convict told him that "the Fortunes would go down in a blaze of fury." Looks as if the first stop in the Lockhart Revenge Train will likely be the Double Crown Ranch. Family patriarch Ryan Fortune is said to have installed a security detail to put Fort Knox to shame—but what would we expect from a

mogul whose family is more precious than solid gold?

Enough doom and gloom... here's the latest on Red Rock's most romantic family. *The Tattler* has the scoop on dreamboat bachelor Brody Fortune. When this Aussie tycoon "met" his new *pregnant* secretary, Jillian Tanner, there was an undeniably familiar, lusty glint in his steel-gray eyes. Could all that eye-popping be about her exceptional *steno* skills...?

THE F⬡RTUNES OF TEXAS™

 Meet the Fortunes of Texas

Brody Fortune: The powerful executive's new secretary was his long-lost love…and he was shocked! The girl he remembered was now a woman—and a single mother-to-be. Could the truth about the past heal their wounded hearts and make them a family of three?

Jillian Tanner: She thought she'd outgrown thoughts of happily-ever-after, yet when she found herself face-to-face with the only man she'd ever truly loved, she wondered if she could convince Brody that he could bestow his heart on her once more.

Matilda Fortune: This dutiful daughter longed to get away from the watchful eyes of her overprotective brothers. Would the blossoming beauty ever meet a man brave enough to hold his own with her brothers…and sexy enough to sweep her off her feet?

THE EXPECTANT
Secretary

LEANNA WILSON

Silhouette Books

Published by Silhouette Books

America's Publisher of Contemporary Romance

Special thanks and acknowledgment are given to
Leanna Wilson for her contribution to
THE FORTUNES OF TEXAS series.

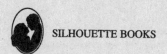 SILHOUETTE BOOKS

THE EXPECTANT SECRETARY

ISBN 0-373-21741-2

About the Author

THE FORTUNES OF TEXAS™

LEANNA WILSON

A native Texan, Leanna Wilson was born and bred in Big D, but she's a country girl at heart. She loves visiting her parents' ranch in east Texas, whether she's helping to herd cattle or simply sitting by the lake, and she enjoys vacationing in the Rocky Mountains, dreaming up new plots by the side of a rippling brook.

More at home dreaming up stories than writing lesson plans, Leanna gave up teaching to pursue writing. Once she began putting her stories onto paper, it didn't take her long to publish her first Silhouette Romance novel, *Strong, Silent Cowboy,* which won the Romance Writers of America's Golden Heart Award. "That was a summer I will never forget," Leanna says. "I sold my first book, got married to my not-so-silent city-slicker husband and after a fabulous honeymoon in England and Scotland had to go to Hawaii, where I won the Golden Heart Award."

Besides writing Silhouette Romance, Harlequin Temptation and Harlequin American Romance novels, Leanna keeps busy with her two children. She teaches a writing class and leads a book club at the senior center near her home. But mostly she enjoys spending time with her growing family.

To Matrice—a terrific editor!

One

"Jillian, you're the luckiest woman in all of San Antonio!"

Lucky? Jillian Hart Tanner squelched her disbelieving laughter. As far as she was concerned, life had dealt her a pathetic hand. She certainly had the sorriest love life. In fact, she'd never felt lucky at anything, least of all on this day as she sat alone at a table in the third-floor lounge of the Fortunes TX, Ltd. high-rise. She snapped a saltine cracker in two and placed half of it in her mouth rather than respond to the data entry specialist's envious statement.

"I'd say in the whole U. S. of A." Alice from accounting poured another packet of sweetener into her coffee and stirred it in with a skinny red straw. "I got a glimpse of your new boss first thing this morning. My, my, my!"

Pretending not to care about the conversation spinning around her, Jillian tried to ignore the nervous fluttering of her heart. She tried to swallow, but the cracker stuck in her throat. Her stomach had been on the verge of mutiny all morning. She clasped her trembling hands under the table.

"You saw him, too?" Kathy from data entry adjusted her wire frames as if preparing for a better glimpse of the newest Australian import of the Fortune clan should he waltz through the door.

"Have mercy!" Alice fanned her face with her hand. "If *he* was *my* new boss, I'd be fired for chasing him around the desk, sure as the world. But, Lord, it'd be worth it."

Kathy laughed. The sound grated on Jillian's nerves and she gritted her teeth. Why couldn't her new boss have been anyone other than Brody Fortune? Just the thought of the tall, rugged Aussie was enough to make Jillian's pulse surge as if she'd been jolted with electricity.

"If you play your cards right, Jill," Alice added, "you could end up the newest Mrs. Fortune."

Jillian's heart pinched tight. Yeah, right. She'd had her chance with the too eligible bachelor once. A long time ago. The odds of that happening then or now were as remote as winning the Texas forty-million-dollar lottery. Besides, she wasn't interested in the dubious distinction of Mrs. Fortune anymore.

Glancing at the digital clock on the wall, she folded her brown paper sack, stuffed it inside her purse and pushed away from the table. "The last thing I need," she said, "is a man."

After all, her husband—her scallywag of a husband…her deceased husband—had put her in extreme financial straits. Resulting in this awkward predicament. One more thing to blame on James.

She squared her shoulders as she left the lounge and headed for the elevator. It didn't matter who her new boss was. This was business. It was her job. One she desperately needed. She didn't have the time, the need, or the luxury of an office romance.

Especially with Brody Fortune.

He'd broken her heart once. Eons ago. In a faraway land. She wouldn't let it happen again.

Oh, Lord. Her heart fluttered, leaving her light-headed. She put a shaky hand to her forehead. *What have I agreed to?*

Had she really been given a choice? She'd been offered a promotion. How could she refuse? Especially when she needed the extra money the raise would afford. Straightening the hem of the suit jacket she'd borrowed from her sister, she reminded herself that any luck she had would be focused on getting this job. She had to make the most of it. She couldn't afford to lose it and waste precious days, weeks or months looking for another. Even if her boss would be Brody.

The elevator doors opened on the seventeenth floor. Sucking in a thin breath, she clutched her purse in her hands and approached the receptionist's desk. "I'm Mr. Fortune's new assistant." Jillian spoke with more confidence than she felt. "Is he ready to see me?"

A wave of uncertainty nearly knocked her over. Maybe she should have asked if *she* was ready to see *him.* Definitely not!

Pushing a strand of dark hair behind her ear, the woman gave her a tolerant smile. "Which Mr. Fortune?"

"B—" Jillian cleared her throat. "Brody." His name tasted tart on her tongue. How long had it been since she'd spoken it out loud? When she'd returned from Australia ten years ago, she'd never mentioned him—or her humiliation—to anyone, even her sister. "Brody Fortune."

"Ah." The receptionist gave a knowing nod. "He's in the boardroom. I'll buzz him." Before Jillian could protest, the brunette pushed a button on her monitor.

"Yes," a rough-hewn voice that brought back too many memories snapped over the speaker.

Jillian's heart began to pound. Her fingers clasped her purse.

"Your assistant's here. Shall I send her in?"

"Right. Go ahead." That rugged Australian accent had once made her temperature skyrocket. But now it plummeted, left her cold.

She couldn't do this. She couldn't. Not after… Oh, God!

The receptionist gave her a brief nod. "Down the hall and to the right. It's the fourth door on the left."

Jillian's knees wobbled as she walked down the hall. Her pulse throbbed in her ears. Had Brody requested her? No, he couldn't have. How would he have known that she worked for his family's company or that she'd moved to San Antonio from Amarillo? She wouldn't have taken this job in the first place if she'd known Brody was in any way connected to the Fortunes of Texas. Or if she'd believed there was even the remotest possibility that he would come here.

As she touched the brass door handle, her fingers became numb, her limbs ice-cold. What could she expect, seeing him again? She wanted to bolt rather than open the door, but she knew she had no choice. She could face Brody again. She could. Without regrets. Without her temper getting the best of her. After all, he was the one who should be ashamed. Not her. Besides, it had been ten years since they'd dated. Ten long years. She'd lived through much worse than a broken heart.

And she could survive this.

Before she could turn the knob, the door jerked open, practically pulling her inside the boardroom. She caught glimpses of a plush honey-colored carpet and a table as large and gleaming as a brand-new Cadillac. And Brody.

Her heart froze in midbeat. The room had been decorated to give the Fortunes home-court advantage in their high-powered meetings. But it wasn't the posh decor that threw Jillian off center. It was those too familiar chrome-gray eyes. He was the company's secret weapon, the ace negotiator, a top-notch executive.

Immediately, she saw changes in him. The difference between boy and man was as stark as black versus white. Where once he'd had fiery eyes with a spark of mischief, they were now as cold and hard as nickel-plated steel.

His gaze met hers. A whirlwind of emotions churned in the silvery depths. Surprise, confusion, recognition mirrored the turbulence inside her. "What the hell...?"

Jillian's heart jackhammered against her breastbone. Her lungs compressed. "Excuse me for intruding—"

"Come on in, Jillian." Dawson Prescott, the top financial analyst for Fortune TX, Ltd., the man who'd hired and promoted her, waved her into the boardroom.

"What are you doing here?" Brody blurted.

"I'm your new assistant." Her voice harbored a distinct waver. Vaguely aware of others watching, listening, she flicked her gaze toward the head of finance. Not wanting to advertise the fact that she and Brody shared a past, she filed away any potentially sharp retort. Her thoughts spun crazily. How should she handle this? Professionally. Facing Brody again, she stuck out her hand. "I'm Jillian Tanner."

For a flash of a second Brody's sculpted features revealed the young man she'd once known, exposed his astonishment. Then he shuttered his emotion with the blink of an eye.

Once again she had a hard time recognizing him. Not because his features had changed. His hair was the same midnight-black, sinfully dark, temptingly wavy. But his face had lost the softness of youth; his voice, the laughter; his eyes, the vulnerability. He was all hard angles and edges. His shoulders, accentuated by the gunmetal-gray of his suit with its knifed creases, were as broad as the Texas borders. He looked like a Stepford corporate exec, straight out of the pages of the *Wall Street Journal,* except for the slash of a red tie and the rebellious length of hair that curled over his starched white collar.

She almost breathed a sigh of relief. Almost. If he'd

been the same young man she'd known so well in college she might have had a hard time resisting his charm. But now he reminded her too much of James. The cold memories of her marriage wrapped around her like a wet blanket. Looking into Brody's emotionless eyes, she knew she could never forget how he'd treated her, either.

"You two know each other?" Dawson stepped forward.

Jillian dropped her hand to her side. Obviously, Brody wasn't willing to pretend they'd never met. Anxiety made her temples throb. Dragging her gaze away from Brody, she heard blood roar in her ears. So much for keeping their past in the past. Taking the initiative, she said, "We attended Winslow College together."

"I'll be damned." Dawson gave a chuckle. The attractive financial analyst ran his fingers through his light brown hair. "I hope you're not old lovers or anything."

As if ice cubes slid down her spine, she shivered.

"No," Brody answered. His knowing look speared Jillian. "We weren't."

His hardened tone grated against her nerves. What did he have to be irritated about? Thank God, she'd wised up before he'd made another conquest. She and Brody had come close to becoming lovers. So close. Before she'd learned she wasn't the only woman he was dating or taking to his bed. Remembering the pain and humiliation, Jillian felt her blood congeal. Her stomach lurched and she pressed her lips together.

"Just old friends?" Dawson quirked a skeptical brow, then shrugged. "Good, then I picked the right woman for the job. One of the reasons I chose Jillian was for her experience in Australia. But I had no idea you two would know each other."

Dawson moved to the open doorway. "She'll be an asset in this merger. She's got a good head for numbers." He stepped between them and out the door. "I've got a departmental meeting. I'll let you get reacquainted."

Jillian gave a nod of agreement but wished she could find her desk, sit and put her head between her knees before she keeled over. Her insides fluttered with uncertainty.

"Brody," Dawson added, "give me a buzz if you have any questions. Jillian should be able to get you all the information you need. I want this merger to go as smoothly as possible."

"Thanks, mate." Brody waited for Dawson to turn the corner down the hallway before leveling his gaze on Jillian. Where once he'd been friendly and accepting, he was now distant, seemingly sizing one up as if to calculate their worth. She sensed he considered her a liability.

A long pause pulsed between them before he said, "How are you, Jillie?"

His rugged accent made her name sound exotic, sensual. She remembered his nickname for her, and her skin tingled. "Fine." She crossed her arms over her chest. "I'm fine. And you?"

He leaned against the doorjamb and mirrored her stance. "I'm curious."

She felt as if the air had been sucked right out of her body. She couldn't stop herself from asking, "About?"

"You bailed out of Australia right fast."

She released a pent-up breath. Her shoulders slumped with sudden fatigue. What was the point of rehashing their relationship? "Brody, it's been a long time."

"Then the next thing I know," he continued, ignoring her statement, "I receive a letter telling me you'd married. Did you leave because you missed that bloke... What was his name?"

"James." She made her tone neutral.

"Did you miss him so much?"

Leaving Australia had been the right thing to do. Brody had made her feel worthless...used. She'd been all alone, feeling as if she had no one to confide in, but when she'd called to share her woes with her mother, she'd learned of her mother's sudden stroke. Her mistake had come after she'd returned home when she'd sought the comforting arms of her high school sweetheart. It wasn't until after her marriage to James that she'd truly understood the meaning of lonely.

"I wrote the letter," she said, anger tinting her words, "because I thought you would want to know." She hoped to end this conversation as an uncomfortable heat enveloped her.

"Yeah, right." His cynical tone nettled her. He took a step toward her. His casual stance changed. Suddenly his gaze was hot, intense. A nervous vibration rippled through her, making the back of her neck prickle. "But you didn't think," he said, his voice rough, "that I'd want to give you—" his mercurial gaze focused on her mouth "—a goodbye kiss?"

She gritted her teeth and squared her shoulders. When she'd realized she'd made a mistake marrying James, she'd wanted to reach out to Brody because she still loved him. Even after he'd broken her heart. Yet she'd also wanted to punish him. "If you don't think you can work with me, Brody, fine." She shoved away her regrets and buried them beneath other painful experiences. "I'll let Dawson know you need a different assistant." She turned to go, anger pumping through her veins. No job was worth this.

"Jillie." He grabbed her arm, spun her back around to face him. "Wait. Just tell me why. Dammit! Why'd you bail?"

His hand curled around her wrist, his touch as warm and familiar as an old flannel shirt. Yet his grip wasn't soft or cozy. It felt more like a harsh, ever-tightening vise. A quick flash of heat made her scalp tingle, her skin flush. Stiffening her resolve against him, remembering how he'd hurt her, how used she'd felt, she jerked her chin upward in challenge.

He leaned toward her, piercing her with his blunt gaze. He stood so close that the bold masculine scent of his cologne wrapped around her, captivating, cloying, confining. Blood drained out of her head and pooled in her feet. His face blurred. A whirring noise inside her head made her ears ring.

"Brody, I—" Her words slurred together. Her knees buckled. She reached for him and missed. Her hand swiped at the space between them, catching only air. A swirling vortex of colors spun her around and around. Until she felt herself falling...falling...

Stunned, Brody watched as Jillian began to crumple like a paper doll. Without measuring the consequences, he knelt to grab her before she hit the carpet. He cradled her limp body in his arms.

He looked around for help...for someone. No one was in the hallway. Turning, he sought a place to set her down. The conference table? The floor? A chair? *Damn! Now what?*

She lifted her hand to push him away—or clutch at him, he wasn't sure which. As if in slow motion, her hand fell, heavy, lifeless, across her stomach. He noticed the soft rise and fall of her breasts. Okay, she was breathing. Still, she was definitely unconscious.

Panic seized him. *You, fool!* he cursed himself. *You pushed her to this. You pushed too damn hard!*

"Jillie?" Concern edged his voice as he gave her a light shake.

Pale and placid, her features frozen, she looked almost peaceful. Her shimmery blond hair splayed out across his shoulder. She stirred, a jerky movement, as if she were struggling to climb back to consciousness.

Not knowing what else to do, he lifted her into his arms and carried her toward the conference table. Her slight frame felt as light as a biscuit his mother used to make. Her eyelids fluttered open. Once more he was struck by the vibrant blue-green color. The rich, vivid hues reminded him of the Coral Reef, beautiful to view, but sharp and dangerous.

Why couldn't you leave well enough alone? Why can't you get her out of your mind? And heart?

That's one reason he'd agreed to come to Texas. He'd needed to see her again, needed to for his own survival. So he could go on with his life. Without her memory haunting him. Without his desire for her consuming him.

"Jillie," he repeated. He'd used that nickname today, hoping to irritate her, hoping to hurt her as she'd hurt him so long ago. Memories assaulted him like a cyclone, sweeping in and destroying the protective walls he'd erected. His gut clenched.

"Jillie!" he demanded. "Wake up." He had to put her down and get help.

Before he could move, she shifted restlessly, arching her back against his arm and blinking against the harsh light. "I—I'm okay."

"I've got you." His arms tightened around her shoulders and beneath her legs.

She pushed a lock of honey-blond hair behind her ear but it fell back to curl just below her earlobe, softening the squareness of her jaw. "I'm okay," she repeated, her voice weak and unsure. "Put me down."

"Not till I'm positive you're all right." He did as she requested and lowered her into a buttery-soft leather chair. "I'll call for medical help."

"N-no." Panic stretched her voice into a squeak. "I'm fine. Really." She clutched the sleeve of his jacket. "Please, Brody." The plea in her voice and the insistence in those startling blue-green eyes made him doubt his better judgment.

But then, she'd undermined his sanity for years. When he'd learned his father's half brother lived in Texas, when they'd decided to merge the family's two companies and he was needed here, he'd come with an ulterior motive. To see Jillian again.

He'd called her several months ago, reached her at her home in Amarillo to tell her he was coming. But something had been wrong. She'd sounded so far away, so distant, so sad. Maybe it had been the thousands of miles or simply the ten years deeper and wider than the oceans separating them. He'd hoped just hearing her voice would prove to him once and for all that he was over her. But it had done the exact opposite.

He'd known then he'd had to find her. Even though she'd hung up on him, cutting him off before he'd had a chance to tell her he was coming to Texas. Now she was here. In San Antonio. In his arms.

"Something could be wrong," he said to her, having the same anxiety as that day he'd briefly spoken to her over the phone, the same panic he'd experienced ten years ago when he'd gone to pick her up for a date and discovered she'd left for America. Something was wrong. Or maybe he was the one who needed help. "You should be seen by someone."

She shook her head. "It's my fault. I didn't have time to eat this morning. It's just low blood sugar. That's all."

He studied her for a moment, his gaze flicking over her from head to toe, noting the softer curves where once she'd been skinny with the flat lines and planes of a girl. Now she was a woman. And his reaction was that of a man.

"We really should call somebody." She unnerved him, as no lawsuit or high-profit business deal could.

"N-no, please. Really, I'll be all right. I just need a minute." She touched her hand to her forehead. Her hands were delicate and soft. He had a sudden memory of her smoothing her palms over his chest and sifting her fingers through his hair.

Heat rushed through him. He shook loose the memory and focused on her. Here and now. She looked so pale, so fragile. He had an overwhelming urge to protect her. Her soft, floral fragrance floated up to meet him. He knelt beside the chair, looping an arm behind her. Her lips were parted, vulnerable, tempting. He remembered their sweetness. He remembered too damn much.

"You scared the hell out of me," he said, his voice as rough as the raw emotions coursing through his veins.

"I'm sorry. I'm all right."

Was she? Was he? Seeing her again, he knew he'd never fully recover. Anger snapped inside him. Why couldn't he forget her? What was it about Jillian Hart…Tanner?

He tipped up her chin, lifting her gaze to his. Her skin was as smooth as a rose petal. He'd been with more beautiful women. Women he'd dated to try to erase Jillian from his mind. But no woman had come close to her. And he somehow wanted to make her pay for all the suffering and sleepless nights she'd caused him. Staring into those troubled eyes of hers, he felt himself falling...and he could almost forget she was married. To someone else.

"Are you really sorry?" His voice was intentionally cutting for she'd so easily sliced a piece out of his heart.

She didn't answer. His gaze slipped to her hand, still folded around his lapel. She wore no wedding ring, no declaration of her married status. Questions plagued him. Questions he didn't take the time to have answered.

An overwhelming, irresistible urge grabbed him and wouldn't turn him loose. He wanted her to be sorry. Sorry she'd left. Sorry she'd hurt him. Sorry she'd shown back up in his life. He wanted her to know exactly what she'd missed. He wanted her to know, for one second, what she could have had with him.

He kissed her then, hard, fast, relentless, claiming her mouth, blocking out his anger, his pain, his concern. He didn't want to care about her anymore. He had to get over her. Once and for all.

He kissed her as he once had, as he wished he'd been able to ever since. It was a lusty kiss to make her regret leaving him for the rest of her days. Feeling her soft lips, her mouth opening to him in surprise, all the pent-up pain inside him subsided, replaced by pure, red, pulsing desire. He focused on her mouth, their heat, his need.

Hell! What have you done now?

Before she could slap him, before he did something more that he knew he'd regret later, he broke away. Pulling back, disgusted at himself for kissing her, and at her for kissing him back, he sucked in a deep, ragged breath. "I shouldn't have done that."

She released his lapel, her fingers curling toward her palm. "No," she said, her voice as shaky as his resolve to never let that happen again, "you shouldn't have."

He was in big trouble. He wanted her just as much as he had when they were twenty. Maybe more. Definitely more.

How the hell was he going to work with her every day?

His brain felt fuzzy, stunned by his need, his foolishness. *She's married, you fool!*

He pushed to his feet and gave himself some much needed breathing room by walking to the door. "That won't happen again."

"Was that the goodbye kiss you said I owed you?" she asked, her voice girded with anger and steel.

"No. That was just one more mistake."

Two

Mistakes. Jillian knew all about mistakes. And becoming Brody's assistant ranked right up there as one of her dumbest.

"Easier said than done," she commented two days later with what she hoped was a pleasant if not awkward smile.

Brody's gaze snagged hers, held her motionless. She knew the extensive report he wanted would be easier to write than trying to ignore the way he affected her. Or maybe it was that darn kiss. It had knocked her socks off. She couldn't seem to put it out of her mind. Every time she looked at Brody, at his strong jaw, his firm, supple lips, she remembered. And her body vibrated with…anger, she firmly decided.

She stared at the financial report lying on the desk between them, but her senses remained hypnotized by Brody. He smelled of zesty soap and subtle cologne. He looked like a model straight out of the pages of *GQ* magazine. His conservative, expensively tailored suit hinted at the well-honed physique underneath. Danger lurked in those mysterious gray eyes. She had an alarming urge to comb back the thick black lock that curled carelessly over his forehead.

Stop it! she warned herself. *You don't want Brody. You certainly don't need him.*

But it was much easier to tell herself to forget the texture of his mouth on hers, the desire he'd stirred inside her with that kiss, than to actually erase it from her memory. Her skin still tingled.

Before that kiss, a part of her had felt dead inside. She realized now, in retrospect, she'd felt that way for a long time. Maybe she always had.

When she'd been a child, she'd often felt as though she were sleepwalking through life. Nothing had seemed real. Everything had lost its vibrancy the day her father had walked out on her family. She'd felt as if she lived in the black-and-white portion in *The Wizard of Oz.*

Then she'd met Brody. Suddenly her world had become alive, vivid with Technicolor hues. He'd given her hope through his easygoing manner, his trustworthiness and his love. When she'd learned about Gail, all that had changed. Her world had paled once more.

She'd been numb the day she'd married James, unable and unwilling to feel, but now she knew something inside her had died then. She'd given up on love. On romance. Maybe even on life. She'd traded her soul for security and received nothing but heartache in return.

Strangely, the day James had made her a widow she'd been set free. But not free or desperate enough to want Brody back.

Brody's kiss had zapped her like an electric current to the heart. The sensations that had coursed through her caused more pain than pleasure. It would be easier, she decided, so much easier, if she still felt nothing.

"I didn't say it'd be easy, Jillie," Brody said in that sexy Aussie accent that made her heartbeat quicken. "But it's necessary."

She nodded. "I'll get right on it." She shifted to her left foot, propping her hip on the edge of his solid oak desk, leaning away from him, not wanting to accidentally brush shoulders. Or anything else. "When do you want the report?"

"Next week should be fine. That'll give me a couple of days to look it over before my meeting with the attorneys." His spontaneous smile curled her toes.

Her hand fumbled with the pen she held. It fell and rolled across his desk. He caught it and handed it back to her. Embarrassed by her own clumsiness, she took it, carefully avoiding even the slightest touch.

"Okay, then." She stood on both feet and rounded the corner of his desk.

He caught her arm. Her nerves electrified.

"Jillie?" he said, his voice deepened, intriguing and alarming her at the same time.

Unnerved by his touch, by her own conflicting emotions, she faced him, but this time she refused to meet his scintillating gaze. Pretending to search for some monetary figure, she riffled through the stack of papers she carried. *Get a grip on yourself, Jillian.*

"Did you eat breakfast today?" he asked.

Her chin lifted, her pulse charged. "What?" Surprised by his question, she asked, "Why?"

"I don't want my assistant fainting every day." His

eyes narrowed and he studied her face. "You look…" His pause made her too aware of how much his opinion mattered. Why did she have the feeling he wasn't about to say she looked ravishing? "Pale," he finally said, his voice filled with concern.

"I'm fine." But she wasn't.

"Are you sure?" He closed the gap between them.

"Y-yes." Her voice vibrated with uncertainty.

He bracketed her shoulders with his hands, rubbing, chafing her skin beneath the thin jacket separating his skin from hers until she thought he might start a fire inside her. "You're a bundle of nerves."

"I'm fine," she protested, and took a step back.

He released her but leaned closer, his warm, clean scent surrounding her, his minty breath caressing her ear. She could see nothing beyond his wide shoulders that were covered by the metallic-gray suit. "Do I make you nervous?"

"N-no." She glared at him. Shocked, horrified, irate at his perception, at the truth pounding in her chest, she refused to admit it even to herself and snorted her derision. Oh, God! She actually snorted. A burning heat stung her cheeks. "Of course not."

"Good." He touched her elbow and wild sensations shimmied down her spine. "I wouldn't want what happened the other day…" He paused, inclining his head, dropping his voice to a husky whisper, reminding her of the primitive, erotic kiss they'd shared.

Just what she needed—another reminder! Her stomach tumbled over itself. She should have eaten breakfast. But the thought of even dry toast had made her feel green around the edges.

"...to get in the way of our work," he finished.

"It won't." She wouldn't—couldn't—let it. Because she needed this job too much. A whole lot more than she needed Brody Fortune. Or empty promises.

"A swanky joint you've got here, mate."

The strange voice jerked them apart. Brody looked past Jillian toward the door to his office and an instant grin split his chiseled features. Jillian spun around to see who had intruded on them in such a compromising situation.

"C'mon in, Griff." Brody brushed past her, his arm grazing her shoulder, reminding her how close they'd been standing. Way too close. He clapped the man's shoulder.

"They must think you're important around here." The man had the same Australian accent as Brody, but his voice didn't make her temperature rise. He glanced around the office, tastefully decorated in bold, opulent colors that matched Brody's personality.

The stranger's gaze landed on her. He had nut-brown eyes that looked as if they were shadowed with wariness. "Griffin Fortune."

Another Fortune. Just what she needed. What had they all done? Swarmed the border? Defected? She wished they'd all go back to Australia and leave her alone.

"This is Jillian Hart—"

"Tanner," she corrected Brody.

She noticed Brody's smile harden into a scowl and took pleasure in his lips thinning, the brackets around his mouth tightening. He turned his attention back to his brother. "Have a seat, Griff."

She remembered Brody telling her about Griffin once, so many years ago. He hadn't been born a Fortune, he'd been adopted by Brody's parents and raised on the Crown Peak Ranch in New South Wales. His features were not similar to Brody's. Griffin's hair reminded her of pecan pie, whereas Brody's black hair made her think of rich, dark chocolate. She wondered why she still compared every man to Brody. Irritated at herself, she decided it was only natural since the two men were brothers. But she *had* to stop doing that.

She almost laughed at her latest food craving. She compared everything to food these days. When her stomach rumbled angrily that she hadn't fed it recently, she clutched the folders against her abdomen, hoping to muffle the sound.

Taking this opportunity for a few minutes of privacy to get her thoughts and feelings about Brody under control and her mind back on work, she headed for the outer office.

"Jillie?" Brody stopped her.

"I know, two cups of coffee. I'll be right back with them."

He shook his head. "That's not what I meant."

She paused with one hand on the door, eager for escape.

Slanting a glance at his brother, Brody gave a slight what-the-hell shrug then pulled a white lunch sack from behind his desk. He brought it to her. "Here."

Confused, she stared at the sack. "What do you want me to do with this?"

"It's for you." He lowered his voice to a husky whisper and cut his eyes toward Griffin who sat in the copper-colored suede chair opposite Brody's desk.

"Me? But what—"

"It's a bagel," he answered before she could finish her question. "Eat it. I can't have you fainting anymore." He turned on his heel, dismissing her, and walked back to his desk.

His words were brusque, but the sentiment surprised her. It was a simple gesture. Logical, even. But somehow the sweetness of it touched her.

"I'll be back with that coffee," she muttered.

She closed the door behind her and sank into the chair at her desk. Slowly she opened the paper sack he'd given her. A warm, yeasty scent rose to greet her. Her heart fluttered like a butterfly's wing beneath her breastbone.

He'd remembered. Oh, God, he'd remembered that she loved blueberries. When was the last time a man had given her something? When had a man looked out for her welfare? Or even tried to please her? Hot tears scalded the backs of her eyes.

She sniffed. Hormones, she thought. That's all it is. She wouldn't give in to the weak emotions. She certainly wouldn't allow Brody back into her heart.

"Oh, shoot," she mumbled to herself. "I forgot to get the coffee." She pushed herself up from her chair.

Maybe the blueberry bagel was a peace offering. Fine. She could accept it for that. But nothing more.

She knew Brody was the love-one, love-'em-all kind of man. Too much like James. And definitely not the kind for her.

"Some assistant you have there," Griffin commented, templing his fingers in front of his mouth to hide a smirk. "What's she assisting you with?" His broadening grin aggravated Brody.

"Merging these two companies. That's all."

"Uh-huh. I can see you've got a merger—" he winked "—of some kind on your mind."

Brody frowned and opened a file folder in front of him. "How's everything at the Double Crown?"

"A cyclone of activity."

Glancing up from the accounting profile, Brody leaned back in his chair. "The wedding have things stirred up?"

"Our big brother sure got lassoed by that sheila. Reed's making everybody bend over backward to make this wedding a blasted fairy tale. Guess I can't blame him. Mallory's some woman."

Brody chuckled at his older brother having finally been bitten by love. "She'd have to be to handle Reed."

A discreet knock on the door signaled Jillian's return. She carried in a tray with two cups of steaming, fragrant coffee along with packets of sugar and cream. After depositing the tray on the table beside Griffin, she retreated without a word. Or a look in Brody's direction. He couldn't help but watch her petite hips rock from side to side in a subtle alluring fashion.

He wondered if the blueberry bagel had reminded her of their carefree college days, of lazy naps beneath a eucalyptus tree on campus where they'd kissed and shared their dreams. When he'd decided to stop on his way to the office and pick up a couple of bagels this morning, he'd remembered her penchant for blueberries and the time he'd bought her an ice-cream cone.

His insides had roiled like a broiler as he'd watched her lick the creamy concoction with the tip of her pink tongue. She'd smiled at him seductively, her mouth tilting on one side, a pale blue mustache above her upper lip. Unable to resist, he'd stolen a quick kiss, tasted the sweet tartness on her lips, and the memory still lingered in his mind, whipping his appetite and desires into a frenzy once again.

"Looking for one yourself maybe?" Griff asked after Jillian had again closed the door behind her.

"What?" Brody jerked his attention back to the present.

"Looking to make it a double wedding?"

"Hell, no." He slapped his tie against his abdomen and crossed his arms over his chest. "What can I do for you?"

"I thought it was the other way around. Didn't you have something you wanted me to do for you while we were all here in Texas? Or has your new assistant made you forget about that woman from college you wanted me to find?"

Brody's shoulders tightened. He cleared his throat. "It's not important anymore. I have too much work to do. No time to think about sheilas."

Only Jillian.

Griff took a long, contemplative gulp of his black

coffee, his brown eyes watching Brody over the rim. "How is the merger going?"

"All right," he answered, ignoring the double entendre behind Griff's words. "I'm thinking of doing some research in a couple of weeks. There's a piece of real estate that's recently come on the market. It borders the north side of the ranch. Could be a good investment. Unless you think I should stick closer to the family and the Double Crown."

Griff frowned, obviously understanding Brody's silent question. "I've got my eye on things."

Brody felt the tension in the back of his neck compress on his spine. "Any word on Clint Lockhart's whereabouts?"

"No."

Shoving back his chair, full of restless energy, Brody rounded his desk and settled one hip on the edge. "I don't like the idea of this criminal on the loose."

"Neither do I. He seems to have disappeared."

"What does the sheriff think?" Brody asked.

"That he's still around. Don't worry. I'm on top of things."

Brody leaned forward, resting his elbow on his knee. "I'm not worried about you, sport."

Griffin nodded. "I know what you're thinking— Matilda."

Shaking his head, Brody pictured his rambunctious, too trusting, younger sister. "She's trouble looking for a spot to happen."

"I've been thinking we need to schedule some activities, keep her busy, so she can't run into the wrong kind of people.''

"You mean, men."

"Yes."

"Not a bad idea," Brody agreed. "She should be fine at the ranch."

Griffin scowled. "Have you seen the way she looks at the cowboys out there?"

He nodded. "When I get back from my one-day trip to check out this property, I'll invite her to San Antonio for dinner or sight-seeing or something."

"You can't let her out of your sight," Griffin warned.

"I don't plan on it."

Setting his coffee cup on the tray, Griffin stood. "Think I'll take in a few sights myself before I head back to the ranch."

"Going souvenir shopping?" Brody asked, knowing his brother had other things in mind.

"More like checking out the cop shop. To see if I can find out any more about this Lockhart fellow."

Brody walked his brother to the door. With his hand on the knob, he said, "Watch your back. Lockhart's dangerous."

"I'd say murdering Uncle Ryan's second wife Sophia put him in that category."

"Now he's desperate."

"I'll be careful." Griffin turned. "If you want, I could have someone do a search in the computer for that woman you were looking for."

"It's not necessary."

Griffin's brow creased. "You already found her?"

"I did." And damn if he knew what to do about Jillian now.

"Hi, honey!" Betsy Keene pulled the door shut behind her as she raced into her trailer home, juggling two sacks of groceries. Breathless, she gave Clint her best smile, hoping he'd be in a good mood, wishing he'd greet her with a kiss.

"You're late." He swigged a gulp from his bottle of beer. From the collection of empty bottles on the table, she knew he'd started drinking earlier than usual. His bare feet were propped on the kitchen table, and he wore only a pair of faded jeans that hugged his narrow hips. "Where you been?"

Betsy flushed as she found herself staring at his lean, muscular chest. Clint's virility made her as jittery as a young schoolgirl. She squashed her disappointment at his sharp greeting and knew she shouldn't have taken the time to redo her hair and makeup in the car.

Hiding her disappointment, she set the sacks on the cracked Formica-topped counter. "The girl taking over my station at the diner was late. Then I needed gas for the car. Stopped off at the grocery store and I had to wait for Annelle Grayson to write her check. She's as old as the hills and it takes her an eternity to sign her name. She has arthritis something awful—"

He slammed his bottle on the table. His blue eyes flashed like heat lightning. "Goddammit!"

She froze. "I'm sorry, honey. Here I am babbling on and you're probably starving. It won't take me but a few minutes to get dinner ready. How does fried chicken, mashed potatoes and gravy sound?''

"I don't care about dinner." He shoved his fingers through his auburn hair, which almost reached his shoulders. He was hard and dangerous. He made her feel wild and careless.

"And I didn't even ask how you were feeling." She pulled a package of chicken out of the grocery sack along with potatoes and enough Granny Smith apples to make a pie. "Is your leg paining you?"

"Hell, yes."

She winced at his gruff tone but maintained a pleasant expression. "I'll fix you a bath after dinner so you can soak."

Her gaze snagged on the wad of cash sitting in the middle of the kitchen table. Her heart jackhammered in her chest, just as it had when she'd snuck onto the Double Crown Ranch and into Clint's cabin almost a month ago. He'd asked her to locate his stash of cash as well as an ID from beneath the floorboard of his old cabin. Now, when he drank too much, he pulled it out of his new hiding place. It gave her a panicky feeling deep in the pit of her stomach. She couldn't bear it if he left her. "Are you going somewhere?"

"Eventually." He grabbed the cash and, lifting his hip off the chair, stuffed the wad into his pocket. His mouth quirked upward on one side and sent her stomach to fluttering. "But not without you, sugar. I'll let you know when it's time."

Again she flushed from head to toe, this time with pure, undiluted pleasure. While she readied the chicken for frying, she imagined a life with Clint, traveling from place to place, making love early in the morning, cuddling in front of a crackling fire on a cold wintry night.

"I got you the San Antonio newspaper you asked for. It's there in one of those sacks." She rolled a chicken leg in flour mixed with seasoning salt.

"Can't you get it for me?" He tipped the bottle against his mouth for a long pull. "I'm laid up here."

"Of course, honey, I'm sorry." She rinsed her hands and dried them on her apron. "Here you go."

He took the folded paper from her. His tanned, calloused fingers brushed hers, and her spine tingled with anticipation. Longing welled up inside her, but he dismissed her with a wink. As she turned back to her raw chicken, he pinched her on the backside. She jumped with surprise and giggled with delight. Maybe tonight he'd be feeling good enough to get frisky.

While she washed and cut the potatoes and set them on the stove to boil, he read the paper, rustling the pages every few seconds.

"Well, now, this is interesting," he muttered.

"What's that?" Glancing over her shoulder, she smiled. The heat from the stove made perspiration dot her forehead. With the back of her wrist, she brushed back a lock of hair. "What did you find?"

"The high-and-mighty Fortunes are about to have a wedding." He rubbed the top of the beer bottle along his jaw, scraping the stubble that had been growing for the last few days. "Interesting. Very interesting."

"Who's getting married?" She moved toward him, wiping her hands on her apron.

"Must be one of them Aussie cousins. And some interior designer."

"I just love weddings!" It had been years since she'd been to one. She didn't know many folks. But that didn't matter. Maybe one day soon she'd walk down the aisle herself. Slanting her gaze at Clint, she wondered if maybe he'd be the one waiting for her, waiting to make her his bride.

"This might be the opportunity I've been waiting for." He slapped the paper onto the table. "We just might have to congratulate the bride and groom on their good fortune." He gave a wild, dangerous laugh that sent a chill of excitement and dread down Betsy's spine.

"Feeling any better?" Amy Fairaday asked, her voice as soft as summer rain.

Jillian leaned back in the recliner and popped another lemon drop into her mouth. She closed her eyes but sensed her sister's careful inspection. "I feel okay if I lie completely still."

"Why don't you take a couple of days off and relax? It might help."

"Believe me," Jillian said with a heavy sigh, "nothing will help." Besides, she couldn't take time off from work. She'd only worked for Brody a couple of days. Anyway, she'd need that time later…in about six months.

"So, what's it like?" Amy settled on the couch, throwing her legs over the arm and propping her chin on her hands.

Jillian slanted her gaze toward her older sister. "What?"

"Being pregnant." A dark shadow hovered in her eyes. "Billy and I had talked about having kids. But he was always too busy. Too busy foolin' around getting another woman pregnant."

Frowning, Jillian wondered why the Hart women had been so unlucky in love. Was it in the genes? Or simply bad luck?

At least one good thing had come out of her own horrible marriage. She touched her lower abdomen. Wonder swelled inside her breast. When she'd first discovered she was pregnant, she'd worried, fretted, cursed her luck. Not because of the baby. But because she'd known her marriage was not a good environment in which to raise a child. She'd considered leaving James but had feared what he would do to her…to the baby. She'd hoped an absent father was better than no father at all.

Then he'd died. It had been an answered prayer. Almost. Except she'd never prayed specifically for her husband's death, never imagined it possible or even wished for something so tragic. She'd simply asked for a miracle. And her luck had changed.

Until she'd run into Brody.

"Being pregnant," she said in answer to her sister's question, "is wonderful." After James's funeral, the shock of her pregnancy had given way to wonder and awe before reality had sunk in. Then she'd worried about finances as her husband's bills and debts rolled in, erasing every cent of the insurance money. But the fears had never for one moment made her regret this baby. Her child would be her new beginning.

"And terrifying." She modified her earlier statement. If it wasn't for her sister's generosity, she didn't know where she'd be living now.

She wondered when she'd feel the baby stir inside of her and hoped it would be soon. Then she added, "And strange."

Amy chuckled. "All that, huh? The 'wonderful' I can imagine. The 'terrifying' is understandable being a single mom. But why 'strange'?"

Jillian laughed for the first time in days. "I've turned into the biggest klutz."

Tilting her head back until her long golden ponytail stretched the length of her spine, Amy laughed. "I don't believe that."

"It's true." She sucked on the tart lemony flavor of the candy in her mouth. "I've never tripped or spilled so much in my life. At the office everyone has started keeping clear of me. The government could declare me a disaster zone at any time. And I can't seem to remember anything. I start to look up a file and I forget what I'm searching for. I've lost my keys twice this week. I guess it's a good thing the baby's attached at this point or I might accidentally forget it somewhere."

"I doubt that." Rubbing her socked feet together, Amy asked, "Want some hot tea?"

"No, thanks. I'm feeling a little better. As long as I keep something in my stomach I'm okay."

"So we need to let you graze all day."

Jillian rolled her eyes. "Great. By my ninth month I'll look like a cow."

"You'll look maternal, glowing, that's all."

She tugged on the band of her skirt that pinched her waist. "Won't be long and I won't be able to fit into any of my clothes. Or yours."

Amy smiled sympathetically. "So when do you think you'll tell your boss?"

Shrugging, she felt her nerve endings vibrate as her thoughts switched to Brody. "Not until I have to. This promotion came with a raise. And I need to keep it. I need to show him I'm indispensable. I don't want to be sidelined just because I'm pregnant."

"But he'll have to learn about it sometime."

"I know." She compressed her lips together. "Just not right now."

"So what's he like?" Amy asked. "You haven't said much about him."

Jillian pulled her bottom lip between her teeth. She hadn't told anyone about her previous relationship with Brody. Sighing, she twisted her fingers together as she remembered the kiss he'd given her. "He's…"

Dark and brooding.

Sweet and generous.

Sexy and too tempting for my own good.

"I don't know," she finally finished.

"The accountant type?" Amy wrinkled her nose.

"Not really."

"Not one of those buttoned-down, Type-A personalities?"

"Well…" It could describe Brody. In a sense. But it didn't encompass all of him. He was certainly more serious now than when she'd known him in college. Of course, he was an executive. He had serious matters to consider.

"What, then?" Amy brushed her bangs out of her eyes. "Does he carry his calculator in his front shirt pocket? Comb long strands of hair over a bald spot? Have crooked teeth? Crossed eyes?"

Trying to envision Brody with any of those maladies, Jillian laughed. "Not at all. In fact..."

"Yes?" Amy prompted, her hazel eyes twinkling with curiosity. "Go on."

A hot sensation that reminded Jillian of Brody's kiss and the heat it had generated made her face burn. "Well, he's..." She couldn't admit that he was sexier than Mel Gibson. Or as intriguing as Crocodile Dundee. "He brought me a bagel at work today."

"That was nice." Her sister's gaze narrowed. "You don't have a thing for your boss, do you?"

"Depends on what you mean by 'thing.'"

Amy groaned. "Oh, no, Jill. This is not a good idea."

"You mean 'wasn't a good idea.'"

Her sister's brow wrinkled with sudden concern. "What happened? Did he make a pass at you? Did you make one toward him?"

Jillian flushed. For a moment she thought she might faint again, but realized she was experiencing a different type of headiness. "Past tense."

"Are you purposefully trying to confuse me?"

"Not really." She shrugged. "Maybe I am." She confused herself. *Forget Brody,* she warned herself. But she knew it was an impossible feat. She popped another lemon drop into her mouth and slid it across her tongue until it lay between her cheek and gum. "Remember when I went to school in Australia?"

Amy nodded.

"Well, I knew Brody—my current boss—then. We, um, sort of dated."

Amy's eyes grew round with disbelief. "You're kidding!"

"I wish I were." She gave a heavy sigh. "It ended badly. But we're trying to go on about our business now. It doesn't mean anything."

"Uh-huh." Amy gave her a sly grin. "I think I know why you're a klutz and forgetting things lately."

Jillian arched an eyebrow.

"It's not your pregnancy, little sister. It's Brody. The new man in your life!"

Three

Brody is not the new man in my life!

Jillian didn't need a man.

Didn't want one.

Certainly not Brody.

She repeated that mantra throughout the rest of the week, especially when she was in his presence. She refused to let him affect her. Negatively or temptingly as he once had. He did not make her feel things she shouldn't. He did not make her feel anything at all.

Carrying a tray with a couple of sandwiches, bags of potato chips and ice-cold drinks, she fortified her resolve and, pushing open the door with her hip, backed into his office. Either he was starving or he was expecting company for lunch.

Brody sat at his desk, his leather chair swiveled to face the panoramic view, and spoke in hushed tones into the phone. From her angle she could glimpse his autocratic profile, his sharply slanted nose, his chiseled jaw. As she moved to his desk she fortified herself to ignore the fact that he'd tugged loose his canary-yellow silk tie and unbuttoned the top button of his starched white shirt, allowing a tuft of dark hair to peek out. Earlier in the day he'd discarded his navy jacket and folded his cuffs up to his elbows. Seeing the dusting of black hair over his tanned forearms hadn't fazed her in the least.

Proving her sister had been wrong in saying Brody was affecting her, Jillian set the tray on his desk, careful to not spill the drinks or knock over the brass picture frame on the desk that held a photograph of a bloodred quarter horse, its shoulders well-muscled, its majestic head turned toward the camera. Probably one of his family's prized studs.

Not at all interested in Brody's hobbies, or that of his family, she turned to go. Out of the corner of her eye she caught Brody's hand signal, motioning for her to wait until he finished his call. Anxious to get back to her desk and the financial report Brody had asked her to generate, to get away from him, she clasped her hands in front of her, shifted from foot to foot and stared out the floor-to-ceiling windows at the view of San Antonio.

The late summer sky shimmered like a turquoise stone, polished and smooth. Sunlight glimmered off a nearby high-rise. Down below, on Kingston Street, live oaks made shady patches in the park with their wide-stretching branches and jade-colored leaves.

"Why don't you have dinner with me?" Brody said into the phone, his voice low, appealing.

Jillian's attention boomeranged back to him. Seesawing a pen between his fingers, making it thump rapidly against his thigh, he elevated her anxiety level several notches. Great, she thought, this was just what she needed. She'd walked in while he was asking a woman out on a date.

Her stomach clenched, roiling with a number of

indiscernible emotions. What did she care? And why did she want to hate the woman?

He cradled the phone between his neck and shoulder, leaning forward as if anticipating a positive response from the person on the other end. A sudden memory flash stung Jillian. She remembered dancing with Brody beneath a starlit sky. Slow, erotic music wrapping softly around them, cocooning them, binding them together in her mind. Her cheek rested against his chest. His chin propped on the top of her head, tucking her safely into the curve of his shoulder.

She slammed the brakes on those memories. Her emotions jackknifed, causing a pile-up inside her as longing, despair and irritation crashed into each other. He'd once made her feel cherished, given her the love and security she'd desperately needed. But the truth had twisted her insides into a heap of mangled metal. She'd never forget—or forgive—the humiliation she'd felt when she'd learned that the entire time he'd been dating her he'd also been seeing an old girlfriend.

Angry with herself for looking back, aching for strong arms to wrap around her with heart-stirring tenderness, she straightened her spine. It was a waste of time to yearn for what had once been between them. What had been only an illusion.

Amy was wrong. She didn't feel anything for Brody. Not anymore.

Proving to herself it didn't matter whom he dated, or what he did with some woman, she busied herself, rearranging his lunch on the tray, folding then refolding his napkin until the paper resembled a handmade fan. She wasn't stalling, wasn't waiting to find out if the woman on the other end of the phone would agree to have dinner with him. She was fixing his lunch.

She tore the paper off a straw and stuck it in his drink, sloshing some of the cola over the side. With each passing moment, her nerves twisted into fine knots. She refused to eavesdrop on his conversation. After all, she didn't care who the woman was. Or what she looked like. It wasn't any of her business.

But she couldn't block out the way he said, "See you then, love."

Furious at herself for paying attention, for the wave of disappointment that knocked her off her feet and the simmer of electricity that made the fine hairs along the back of her neck stand on end, she gritted her teeth. "Your lunch is ready."

She slapped a sandwich down on a paper plate in front of him. Barbecue sauce shot out a slit in the paper covering the sandwich and speckled the front of his shirt. She gasped. "Oh, dear!"

He glanced down at his now spotted shirt, his brows slanting into a frown.

"I'm so sorry." She grabbed a napkin and rounded the desk. She wiped at the mess she'd caused, but the tiny crimson spots smeared. "Oh, no."

His hand folded around her wrist. Tiny fissures of heat spread along her nerve endings. "It's all right," he said, his voice warm, amused, that damn sexy Australian accent reminding her of balmy nights and hot kisses. "Don't worry about it."

Embarrassment branded her cheeks. Her skin tingled where he held her. "B-but I've ruined your shirt."

"I've survived worse." Standing, he continued

holding her arm, his hand encircling her wrist like a heavy, iron band. His height made her tilt her head back to meet his solid-marble gaze. "No worries."

His husky tone sent tiny sparks along her spine and electrified her insides. As quickly as he'd grabbed her arm, he released her and stepped away, leaving her unable to take a breath or clear her head.

With his gaze steady on her, his eyes darkening to the color of charcoal, he began to remove his tie, then untucked his shirt, yanking the tails out of his slacks.

Stunned, she swallowed hard. "W-what are you doing?"

"Changing." Without unbuttoning his shirt, he grabbed the back of the collar and pulled it over his head, turning the fabric inside out and her right along with it.

Blood drained out of her head. Oh, Lord!

With his shirt off, his chest bare, his shoulders were as wide as she remembered. And just as overwhelming. His rugged, outdoor tan had faded with the years, as if he'd been stuck behind a desk too long. But it hadn't diminished the hard, lean edge of his muscles. Or his effect on her.

She tried to focus…on anything but his hard, chiseled body. She shifted her gaze to the brass frame. Maybe that's why he kept a picture of a horse on his desk, to remind him of more carefree days, when he had time to ride in the wind, feel the sun on his face, heat on his skin.

What are you doing? Was she trying to analyze this man? She didn't care why he kept a picture of a horse on his desk. She didn't care who he talked to on the phone, who he dated, who he kissed. She couldn't care less about his faded tan or the way his black hair swirled around his nipples.

But she hated the wisps of heat stirring inside her.

"There a problem?" he asked, his voice as rough as her breath was ragged.

"P-problem?" Her gaze shot back to his face.

"I need a shirt," he prompted. "Grab me an extra, will you?"

She took the shirt he held in his hands and then gave it back to him. What was she doing?

"A clean shirt. I can't go to my meeting this afternoon with barbecue sauce all over me."

"Right." She blinked as if to turn on the ignition in her mind. "You want me to go buy one?"

"Look in the closet." He nodded toward a far door.

"Right. Closet. Shirt. A clean one." Turning on her heel, she moved toward the far door and almost fell over one of the suede chairs.

"Careful," he cautioned, his voice warm and sexy, with a touch of humor that grated on her raw, exposed nerves.

Without glancing back at him, she walked stiffly toward the closet. She gave herself a mental shake. *Get a grip, Jillian! Good God, you're acting as though you've never seen a man half-dressed...er, undressed.*

She'd certainly seen Brody's chest before. But it had been years, ten to be exact. Comparing him now to her memory, she remembered his boyish frame with its slim, wiry lines and buffed, tanned skin. Now his muscles looked cut out of stone. A thick mat of dark hair covered his chest, arrowing down toward the waistband of his slacks. His abdomen had the strength and washboard texture of a swimmer's. He might not lounge in the sun anymore, but he definitely found time to work out.

She squeezed her eyes shut and tried to erase his image. Grabbing a shirt covered in a cleaner's plastic bag, she turned and almost bumped into him. Unbalanced, she blamed the swirling sensations on the baby growing inside her. After all, it had been a couple of hours since she'd nibbled on that blueberry bagel. Brody had made it a habit to leave one on her desk each morning.

Hunger. That's all these feelings were. Pure and simple deprivation.

But what kind? her mind asked. It was definitely physical. But she sensed it was something unrelated to being pregnant. Something hot, sensual. Something related to Brody.

Refusing to look closer at her traitorous emotions, she took a step forward and stubbed the toe of her shoe on the carpet. Before she could fall, Brody reached forward and caught her against his bare chest. The shirt fluttered to the floor. Her hand flattened squarely over his heart. She could feel it pounding, falling far behind the racing of her own. The mat of hair covering his chest was softer than she'd imagined, a provocative contrast to the strength of his muscles, the heat of his skin.

Her gaze collided with Brody's. Heat sizzled between them, like lightning skittering across a summer sky. His eyes were dark, compelling, pulling her to him, making her remember the warmth of his kiss, the passion in his arms. Staring up at him, his arms locked around her waist, she could no longer run from the truth. She wanted—needed Brody to kiss her.

Shocked at her thoughts, at the desire boiling inside her, she curled her fingers toward her palm and pushed away from him. "Um—" She stumbled toward the door. "I'll let you get dressed now. I'll be at my desk. I'll let you know when your lunch guest arrives."

He picked the shirt up off the floor and removed the plastic covering and cardboard from beneath the collar. The play of muscles beneath his taut skin mesmerized her. "I'm not expecting anyone."

"Aren't you?" She glanced at the extra sandwich, chips and soda on his desk.

He shrugged into the heavily starched shirt then fastened each button methodically. "I ordered the extras for you."

"But I—"

"Did you have other plans?" His brow compressed into fine lines.

"No, it's just that…well, I…"

"You don't eat lunch, either?" He winked, giving her heart a lurch.

A smile tugged at her lips but she resisted. Still, his thoughtfulness touched her. Did he notice everything? "Actually, I am starving."

"Good. Then have a seat." He indicated the copper-colored suede chair she'd almost run over earlier then looped his tie around his neck. As he stepped into the private bathroom to tuck in his shirt and use the mirror to adjust his tie, he continued through the open doorway, "I thought we could go over some of those figures while we eat."

Disappointment shot through her, followed by irritation. What did she expect? What exactly had she wanted from Brody? A date? She could have laughed at the absurdity of that thought. This was business. He was her boss. Nothing more.

"Do you like barbecue?" he asked, returning to his desk fully dressed, his tucked-in shirt accenting his trim waist. He unwrapped the paper-covered sandwich and the tangy aroma filled the room.

"Almost as much as chocolate," she answered.

He grinned, and she realized she hadn't seen him smile, really smile, since she'd started working for him. The way the elongated brackets surrounding his mouth creased his cheeks made her toes curl.

"You're a real Texan, then."

"Nothing but." She opened her sandwich and poured an extra amount of sauce over the chopped beef.

"You didn't grow up in San Antonio," he said, taking a bite out of his sandwich.

"That's right. Amarillo." Sensing his unanswered question, she added, "It's in the Panhandle. A good ways from here."

"Were you homesick for Texas?" His pensive gaze made her feel restless inside her own skin. "Is that why you left Winslow so suddenly?"

She almost choked on a bite but washed it down with a deep pull on her soda. Her mind spun. She'd never told Brody why she'd left. Now it seemed too late, too petty, too painful to bring up what should have been forgotten. Even if she'd never gotten over Brody, never forgotten him, never forgiven herself for giving her heart so completely. But she didn't want him to know how he'd hurt her. Not now. Not when it didn't matter.

Reverting to the excuse and truth that she'd given the scholarship board for why she'd returned to the States early from her studies in Australia, she answered carefully, "My mother was sick."

He gave a thoughtful nod. "Your letter said she passed away not long after you returned home."

"That's right." It still gave her a strange, empty feeling that she couldn't pick up the nearest phone and call her mother. She didn't think the gaping hole in her heart would ever close from that traumatic loss. The loneliness had been unbearable during her marriage to James, when she'd longed to call her mother for advice. Now a sharp twist constricted her heart. She couldn't share her pregnancy with her mother, either.

He paused for a moment as if to pay tribute to her long-ago buried mother. When he next spoke, his tone had hardened. "And then you married your old boyfriend."

"Yes. James."

His mouth pulled to the side as if he couldn't make himself say the name. Several moments passed as they each concentrated on their sandwiches. Then he pinned her with a fine-pointed stare. "Has he made you happy, Jillian?"

Startled by the question, by the concern in his voice, her mind spun. Happy? Had James made her happy? Words clogged her throat. Her engagement had made her dying mother happy. The match had pleased James's folks. She wasn't sure what James had wanted. Another conquest? A Stepford wife to help him climb the ladder of success?

And her? What had she wanted? Security? Comfort? Escape from memories...and gnawing pains of regret and loneliness. Had it brought her happiness? No. Her marriage had only made things worse.

It was an answer she couldn't readily admit. Especially to Brody. Her marriage to James had been a mistake from the start. But still the admission tasted bitter.

Instead, she skirted the topic completely with, "James is dead."

Jillian Hart Tanner. A widow?

That description didn't compute. Brody's mind replayed her words over and over, as if trying to make sense of an illogical equation. It seemed simple. But the implications were mind-boggling. Finally the answer clicked and shifted his universe.

She's not married.

She doesn't have a husband.

She's available!

A surge of unreserved, unabashed optimism flooded his soul. His pulse quickened, his blood pumped, hot and fast.

He stared at her, seeing her as he once had, beautiful, intelligent, single. But something in her eyes had changed. Sadness darkened, swirled in those aqua depths like storm clouds. He imagined her tears as she cried for her dead husband. Those tears poured over him, dousing his inappropriate excitement.

You fool, can't you see she's hurting? Can't you be sensitive, instead of thinking of yourself?

Guilt saturated him, made him focus on Jillian. Her pain. Her loss.

"I'm sorry, Jillie." Not sorry that James was dead. He'd never liked James Tanner. Hell, he hadn't even met the bloke. But he'd despised him for taking Jillian away…for marrying the only woman he'd ever loved. "I didn't know."

"It's not something I talk much about."

He nodded. "Doesn't come up in conversations easily, does it?"

She shook her head and stared down at her hands. Her fingers turned white. He wondered if it was a struggle every day for her to wrestle her composure, to combat the anguish.

Like a slap, the truth hit him, the sting resonating through him, making a part of him he'd thought long dead tremble. She'd *chosen* James. Not him. No matter how sharp the truth, he couldn't forget or ignore that fact.

He looked at her from across the desk and read the shadowy pain darkening her eyes. So many questions spun around his mind. How long had she been alone? What had happened to James, a young man of their own age? Too young to die. Too young to leave a beautiful wife.

"When did he…?"

"Two months ago."

"Hell, Jillie." Shock brought the words too fast. "What happened?"

Daintily, thoughtfully, she dabbed at her mouth with a napkin. "An accident. On the road. If you don't mind, I'd rather not talk about it."

Lifting his hand, he wanted to go to her, reach out

to her, hold her. But he knew he shouldn't. He searched his soul but could find no words that might offer solace. He understood the need to turn inward, to protect the shaky walls of dignity.

Slowly he nodded his understanding and cursed himself for causing her more pain. His chest constricted with a raw burning agony for the heartache she must be suffering. He wished he could give her something to cling to for support—his hand, his arms, maybe. But he knew there was no comfort for a broken heart.

And damn if he ever wanted to be Jillian's second choice.

It was the right thing to do, Jillian told herself over the next few days as they entered the last week of September. It was best if everyone, especially Brody, thought she mourned James's loss. She wanted others to think she was a grieving widow. Even if the image she'd created was a blatant lie.

There was no reason to disparage James's memory. No reason to let her wounds from her marriage ooze. She could clean them in private. But she felt as if she were keeping a dark, ugly secret, which made her feel isolated, alone.

And the feeling only grew worse.

Brody was to blame. Every day she worked with him in close quarters, analyzing reports, scheduling meetings. His rugged accent coiled her insides. She caught herself watching him, noticing his hands, his eyes, his smile. Glimpses of her past crept into her unconscious, reminded her of better days, of a time when Brody had made her feel special. It became a constant struggle to remember how he'd also made her feel used, how he'd broken her heart. And why she no longer trusted him.

With long, ambitious strides, Brody walked into his office, a grin as broad as the Palo Duro Canyon lighting up the sharp angles of his face. "You did good, Jillie. Damn good."

Pushing up from her desk she followed him, carrying his phone messages in her hand. "The report helped your meeting with the attorneys?"

"It laid out the strategy perfectly." He set his fawn-colored briefcase on his desk and popped the brackets. "This may end up being the smoothest merger in history."

Pride surged within her. "I'm glad." She handed him his messages. Their fingers brushed, sending an electrical current through her. Crossing her arms, she focused on work. "So what's the next step?"

His gaze softened, making his eyes smoky. "That's what I wanted to talk to you about."

Her enthusiasm kicked into gear. She liked the challenges her new position created for her, taking her mind off her own personal problems. "Whatever I can do—"

"What are you doing this weekend?" His question stopped her short.

Had she mistaken his intent? "Excuse me?"

"This weekend," he repeated. "What are you doing?"

Oh, God! He's asking me out.

Her pulse thrummed at the possibility—at the impropriety, she corrected. Her mind raced. Of course, she couldn't go out with him.

Possible excuses filed into place. But the sorry fact was, she didn't have any *real* excuse. Except that she didn't *want* to see him in anything but a professional setting.

"I, um, well, Brody…" She stuttered to a halt, not knowing how to handle this situation.

She was *not* interested in him. Or anybody else, for that matter. She wondered why that same denial was beginning to sound more and more hollow.

Maybe she should just explain to Brody that it was too soon after James's death. Anyone would understand that. She wouldn't have to explain further. She wouldn't have to lie. Worse, she wouldn't have to confront the truth making her knees weak with need.

Strengthening her resolve, she forged ahead. "Brody, I don't think that's a good idea."

"What?"

"About this weekend."

"You don't?"

"No." She maintained eye contact even when she wanted to look away. She had to be firm. "It's risky. It's…well, the timing is completely wrong."

He rubbed his jaw. "How do you know?"

Biting down on her frustration, she wished he would just accept it and move on. "Isn't it obvious?"

"No. Explain it to me." He folded his arms over his broad chest. "I admit I'm new at this."

New at asking a woman out? She swallowed a laugh. He was the expert. Not her!

"Look, I could make a dozen excuses, but the truth is, I don't have any plans. And I don't want any. If I were to make up something, it would mislead you. Then we'd be right back in the same place. Let me make it as plain as I can. I'm a recent widow. I'm not interested in romance...or anything else. I don't think—''

''I wasn't asking you out.''

Confused, she blinked. ''Excuse me?''

His mouth quirked into a semblance of a smile. He chuckled, but his gaze smoldered like a banked fire. ''But if that's what you want—''

''No.'' Embarrassed heat flared inside her. *What have I done?*

You've made a complete fool of yourself, that's what!

''Let me explain,'' he continued, erasing the amused smile pulling at his lips. ''I'm interested in looking over a piece of property near the Double Crown Ranch. It's actually a winery. I hear there are several vineyards in this part of Texas. It's a growing industry, here, as well as in Australia. I think it might be a good investment for our newly merged company. And it would expand the ranch even more.''

''Oh.'' She couldn't say anything else. She wished she had a magic button that would make her disappear.

''I was hoping you'd go with me. It borders the north side of the ranch.''

''Isn't the Double Crown Ranch kind of large?''

''Approximately five hundred thousand acres.'' He spoke as if that was a drop in an old bucket.

''That could take a while to cross.''

''We have to go around but it should be only a three or four hour drive. You could help gather information for my presentation to the board. But I understand if you're not comfortable—''

"Forget what I said." How could she have been so stupid? The only way for her to not look like a fool was to go with Brody. What had she done? "Please, just forget everything I said."

He quirked a brow. "What are you saying?"

"Basically that I've been a complete idiot. I'm sorry, Brody. I—I…"

"Then you'll go with me? To see the property, that is."

Why did she think she'd regret this? Not for the usual reasons, but because it was now so obvious that Brody wasn't interested in her.

"If you n-need me," she stammered. "I mean, need me for work…for…" Flustered, she tried to mask the sudden twinge of disappointment…and irritation. Why didn't he want to go out with her? That thought placed her in dangerous territory. She shouldn't care what he thought about her. Or if he could ever be interested in her as anything other than an assistant. It shouldn't matter.

But somehow it did.

Four

You're just asking for trouble. Amy's words haunted Jillian as she drove across San Antonio to reach Brody's apartment punctually at nine o'clock the following Saturday morning. She'd suggested they go in her battered Camry, since she knew her way around Texas better than Brody did and they'd have to take back roads to reach the winery. He wasn't the type to willingly turn control over to anyone, but he had reluctantly agreed.

Her palms began to sweat as she turned into the circular drive of the Remington Heights' high-rise luxury apartments. She convinced herself that her rattled nerves were from the snobbish look the valet gave her as she parked outside the sliding-glass door entrance. But she knew the real reason.

Brody.

"Can I help you, miss?" the valet asked, meeting her as she opened her car door.

"I'm here to see a fr—my boss. Brody Fortune."

He squinted down at her, his slicked-back hair reflecting the sun's rays. "Is he expecting you?"

"Yes." What did she look like, a groupie? "He is."

"Very well." Although obviously doubtful, he relented. "If you'll step into the lobby, the receptionist will ring his apartment. In the meantime, I'll drive your car around back.''

Probably so it wouldn't be an eyesore in front of the swanky building. She handed over her keys in exchange for a valet ticket. ''Fine.''

Jillian's nerves chafed raw as she waited for the female receptionist with French-manicured nails and mink-colored hair to ring Brody. In a haughty tone, the woman said, ''Mr. Fortune, pardon me for disturbing you, but there's a woman here who says she has an appointment with you…a…''

''Jillian Tanner,'' she answered the receptionist's silent question.

The woman paused, listening to Brody's response. ''Yes, sir, I'll send Ms. Tanner right up.'' She placed the receiver back in its cradle. ''He said he was expecting you.''

Imagine that!

The woman flicked a contemptuous glance over Jillian's khaki slacks and butterscotch top. ''Take the elevator to the seventh floor. Mr. Fortune is in apartment 7-D.''

''Thank you.'' A satisfied smile pulled at Jillian's lips. She stepped into the oak-paneled elevator, almost relieved that she only had Brody to face.

Before the doors closed, she heard the receptionist mutter, ''Wouldn't have thought *she* was *his* type.''

Well, Jillian wasn't Brody's type. She never had been. Never would be. This was business, she assured herself, and that's all.

When the elevator reached the seventh floor, she walked down an elegant hallway, her steps muffled by the muted brandy-and-forest-green runner that stretched the length of the hardwood floor. Along the way, she passed polished tables decorated with impressive silk flower arrangements, Queen Anne-style armchairs and gold-framed paintings in the tradition of Monet. It didn't take much to remind her that she and Brody were from very different worlds.

She paused at the last apartment and swallowed the rest of her reservations. Why did she feel like a pauper about to enter the king's palace? Staring at the massive twelve-foot-tall door, she felt her stomach twist into a rock-hard knot.

After ringing the bell, she waited. And waited. A few anxious seconds passed, and she glanced at the gold-plated plaque again—7-D. Where was Brody? Hadn't he said for her to come right up?

Allowing another pause, she finally rang the bell again. If he didn't open the door soon, she would retrace her steps. Perplexed, she started to turn away when the door swung open.

Brody greeted her with an embarrassed grin. A shock of black hair fell across his brow, and she resisted the absurd urge to smooth it back into place. In one hand he held a spatula and in the other a smoking skillet.

Jacques Pépin, the famous French chef, he wasn't. But fatally sexy, he was. She felt the impact of his smile clear down to her toes.

"So much for breakfast." His starched white shirt and faded blue jeans seemed as out of place in the opulent surroundings as he would in a kitchen. "We can eat on the way to the vineyard."

"You made breakfast? For me?"

"I know you haven't had anything to eat." He narrowed his gray eyes on her as if suddenly unsure of himself. A rare emotion for Brody, one that made him seem vulnerable, and too appealing. "Have you?"

She'd only had toast earlier, but it seemed like hours since she'd eaten as she was already starving. So far today she'd felt normal, no nausea, no dizziness, until the smell of cremated eggs reached her. Immediately, she reached in her purse for a lemon drop to ease her suddenly roiling stomach.

He scrunched up his nose at the acrid odor. "Doesn't make your mouth water, does it?" Backing away, he said, "Come on in. Let me turn off the stove and we'll head out."

Popping the tart candy in her mouth, she stepped into the foyer, noticing the polished marble flooring, the elaborately carved grandfather clock and the sparkling chandelier. Imagining a host of employees to do his cooking and cleaning, she asked, "You don't cook often, do you?"

"How'd you guess?" He carried their charred breakfast into the kitchen and dumped the ruined eggs into the sink.

Following, she could tell the black-and-white tiles had been spotless before Brody had started breakfast. Bacon grease spattered the stove. Coffee grounds dotted the counter. The percolator sputtered and hissed as coffee flooded the carafe. The robust aroma cleared the cobwebs out of her head.

Smoke set her in action. It curled out of the toaster. Jerking the plug out of the socket, she frowned at the blackened crust. "Maybe I should offer to make you breakfast sometime."

Her gaze collided with Brody's. His eyes smoldered. Her insides simmered. What had she offered? Certainly not what her question had suggested! Having breakfast often implied...

"I—I mean, well..." She wiped her hands on the back of her slacks. "Maybe we should go...leave... before the smoke alarms start going off." Or any other alarms besides the ones inside her head blared. "If you're hungry, we can pick up something on the way." She turned abruptly on the low heel of her sandal and headed toward the door.

Be careful, Jillian, be very careful. Brody is not what you're looking for. A home would be nice, yes. A family, certainly. But a man like Brody? No way! He moves in a fast lane with sporty cars and glitzy women. Not a pregnant mommy-to-be, like you.

Not a problem, she thought. She wasn't interested in Brody any more than he was interested in her. She had everything under control. Especially her hormones. And her emotions.

But she couldn't contain a smug smile a few minutes later as she and Brody walked through the lobby, the receptionist's jealous gaze following their every move.

Watch yourself, Jillian. Don't get too cocky, especially when you have no claims on Brody.

She had once. Or so she'd thought. The memory brought a mixture of pleasure and pain bubbling to the surface.

By the time they'd reached the interstate, Jillian had settled into her role as chauffeur. Her hands gripped the steering wheel with confidence. She kept her gaze on the road and shifted her eyes only to glance at the rearview mirror. Never to look at Brody. Better safe, she reasoned, than sorry.

"Did you finish college here in the States?" Brody asked, trying to make light conversation. He sipped his coffee, which they'd picked up in a fast-food drive-thru.

"No," she answered. "After my mother died, I didn't have the finances." She'd only made it to college at eighteen via a scholarship. After all, her mother had been a hardworking single woman, working odd jobs here and there to pay for Jillian's and Amy's school clothes. There hadn't been extra money for college, especially after Jillian's father had deserted them. During her freshman year at Texas Tech, she'd received another scholarship that had taken her abroad to Australia.

"With your grades and brains, you could have picked up another scholarship." He narrowed in on another of her regrets. "If you'd wanted to."

"I suppose." But she hadn't tried. She'd opted for another type of security. One that had seemed more sure, more solid, more promising than a framed document. "I got married instead." That was her worst regret. Her knuckles turned white as her grip on the steering wheel tightened.

"Did you miss college life?" he asked, continuing his probe.

He was just trying to make conversation, she reasoned. What did she expect? For him to sit like a stone in her car for the whole ride?

"You mean, studying? Partying? Or living far away from home?" She tried to make light of his question, of the disappointment she still felt.

"All three."

Wishing he would have laughed instead of taking her seriously, she shrugged, then paused as she switched lanes and tried to find an answer. "I still study. At least I have since coming to work for you. But I'm enjoying the challenge with all the spreadsheets and financial analyses."

He chuckled. "You're more capable than you think."

A pleased blush crept up her neckline.

"What about the camaraderie, the friends, the hell-raising?" he asked.

She laughed this time. "That kind of craziness I can do without."

"Right. We all have to grow up sometime."

She nodded. Had he? He seemed different, more serious, much more firm. She wasn't sure if that was a positive or negative. Or which side of him was more dangerous.

Keeping the conversation in a safer zone and her thoughts off Brody's appeal, she commented, "After Mom died, I wanted to be as close to home as possible, where things were familiar...and reminded me of Mom, made me feel closer to her."

"I can understand that." His rugged accent lost its earlier humor as his tone dipped lower.

Surprised by his answer, she glanced over at him. A mistake. His smoky eyes clouded her thoughts. "You can?"

"Sure. When something troubling, heartbreaking happens in life, you want to be near those who love and understand you. It gives you a bit of security. Don't you think?"

She nodded, feeling a connection build between them. One she didn't want but couldn't sever, either. How could he understand her? He had a large, loving family. He had more financial resources than she could imagine. He hadn't made the mistakes she had.

"Sometimes," she said, her thoughts drifting back through the years to more carefree days, "I think about the friends I left behind in Australia."

"Do you keep up with anyone?"

She rolled her palms over the padded steering wheel. "When I left, I said goodbye to everyone... everything there."

"Not me." His words were brief, but filled with pain, not anger.

"Brody, don't."

"You could come visit sometime," he suggested. "See those college friends. And anything else you might like."

"Maybe." But she knew she wouldn't. How could she afford it? Why would she want to relive the humiliation and heartbreak she'd suffered there?

"We had good times," he offered like a white flag.

"Some." Memories filed through her mind, tumbling her emotions as if they were a row of dominoes.

"You don't have good memories of Winslow?" His tone deepened, pulled at her, tugged on her heartstrings. "Of me?"

That was her problem. She did have good memories, warm ones, passionate ones of Brody. Those memories had made it doubly hard for her to forget, for her to move on with her life. Too often she'd looked back, compared and contrasted her life with what it could have been. With Brody. And that was always a mistake. Because the man she'd once loved wasn't real. He'd been a figment of her own imagination.

Unfortunately, he still was.

Sensing him watching her, waiting for her answer, she kept her gaze trained on the highway. "Okay, I admit we had some good times."

He seemed to relax, settling back into his seat, drinking his coffee. "Remember you dragging me to that koala park near Sydney?"

Her gaze shot toward him. "'Dragging' you?"

"Too touristy for my tastes. But you wanted to hold a koala."

She chuckled, remembering the warmth of the sun, the heat of his gaze, the laughs they'd shared. "I remember that kangaroo following you like a lovesick puppy."

"The roo had good taste, didn't she?" He gave her a glimpse at the Brody she'd once known and loved. "Were you jealous?"

She choked on her laughter. She'd been jealous of another woman. Gail. She'd always worried she wasn't enough of a woman for Brody. To keep him. To hang on to what they had. And she'd been right.

Shifting in his seat, crossing an ankle over his knee, he asked. "What about my football mates? Quite a few of them asked you out."

She rolled her eyes. "As a joke on you. They weren't serious."

"That's where you were wrong." He gave a mischievous smile. "You didn't know them like I did."

Wanting to switch the conversation off such a provocative topic, she asked, "What happened to all of them?"

"Most are busy working. Or trying not to work too hard."

"What about Mark—?" She snapped her fingers, trying to recall the brawny Aussie's last name.

"Simon?" When she nodded, he laughed. "He married and has four kids. A real family man. Tame as one of those koalas you love so much."

"I can see that happening."

"Sure surprised the hell out of the rest of the gang. Back in college, he was the most likely to pickle his liver."

"He had a kind heart," she said, remembering once sharing her concerns with Mark about loving Brody. "I was fond of him."

"You were?" A jealous tone entered Brody's voice.

"Why haven't you married, Brody?" She turned the tables on him.

He shrugged his broad shoulders. "Haven't found the right lady."

"What about Gail?" She could have kicked herself for asking. But at the same time her hands clenched the steering wheel, her gaze sharpened on the road ahead as she waited for his answer.

"Gail?" His brow furrowed. "Gail Harken? You remember her?"

How could she forget? "She was awfully determined to get a gold band on your left hand."

"Puppy love. Lost touch with her after college. Then I ran into her last year."

Emotions she'd long ago forgotten clogged her

throat. Swallowing hard, she ventured, "You mean, you still see her?"

"Occasionally. She's an investment banker in Sydney. We've done a couple of deals together." He scratched his temple. "She hasn't married yet. Which surprised me because she was so gung ho back in college to get married."

Jillian had an urge to put her hands over her ears. She didn't want to know more. Jealousy pounded through her veins. *It doesn't matter. He's not the man for you, Jillian. Forget him.*

But she knew she couldn't. She felt the attraction pulling her toward him like a powerful magnet. Squaring her shoulders, she focused on the humiliation he'd caused her juggling all his women. She remembered the heartache in her marriage. Hadn't she already made one foolish mistake in that arena? She wouldn't make another.

"You should get married," she stated, her words firm, her voice with a slight quiver. "Maybe Gail is the one for you. Waiting back in Australia."

Maybe then, if he was married and an ocean away again, she could forget him once and for all.

Brody felt nothing inside, only a deep well of emptiness. It was the same overwhelming, engulfing sensation he'd felt the day Jillian had left him all those years before. Now, when he looked toward the future, he saw only a vacuum, sucking him in, swallowing him whole.

Jillian wanted him to marry Gail. She wasn't interested in him anymore. Wasn't that clear? Why was it so hard for him to believe? After all, she'd left him, returned to the States and married James. She *chose* James over him. Plain and simple.

Get that through your thick skull.

Why couldn't he walk away? End this torment? Because there was still something in the way she looked at him, some sparkle, a fissure of heat. He felt it. He knew it. But what could he do about it?

"So you recommend marriage, do you?" he asked, almost flippantly, then regretted his question, remembering her new status as a widow. *Very sensitive, Fortune.*

Before he could take back his words, she answered, "For some. Not for others."

Something in her tone set his nerves on end. "For you?"

"I'm the 'marriage is forever' kind of woman."

His gut clenched. Her marriage to James would never be over. Not even death could sever that bond. Venturing into dangerous territory, he asked, "For me?"

She shot him a glance, then looked back at the highway. "It depends."

"On what?"

"Whether you love the woman you intend to marry and plan to be faithful."

"I did once." He wasn't speaking of Gail. She'd never been the one. Jillian was. Always had been.

But not anymore. She was a widow, married in her mind and heart to a man who was dead. How could he compete?

Years ago, Jillie had told him about her high school sweetheart. James. Just the name made Brody's hand fold into a fist. He'd thought the bloke sounded like a jerk, always taking Jillie for granted, always late for their dates, always telling her what to do, what to wear, who to speak with. But Brody had swallowed his comments and tried to show her through his own actions how a man should treat a woman. How a man should love a woman. But she'd left before he'd finished.

She'd gone back to James.

Jealousy spiked inside him once more. "James must have changed or treated you better. Is that why you chose—married him?"

She snapped her head in his direction. Turbulent emotions swirled like a stormy ocean in the depths of her blue-green eyes. When she looked back toward the road, he realized what he'd done, how far he'd gone.

"Forget I asked that, Jillie." He stared out the passenger window at the sea of green grass. The gentle waves in the contour of the land reminded him of home. Gulping his coffee, he let the scalding liquid punish his tongue and throat.

"I married James," she said, her voice tight, "because I…"

He finished her answer in his own mind—love.

What the hell was love, anyway? The question had haunted him for so long. He'd always believed he'd loved Jillie. But had he? Was it love or obsession for something he couldn't obtain?

When it came to family, he understood the dynamics of love, of caring for others, of sacrificing for them. He'd given up lucrative job offers to help with the family business. His family needed him. And he loved them.

When it came to women, he was clueless. He thought he'd understood love. But when Jillie left suddenly, without a goodbye, without an explanation, she'd jumbled his beliefs into a confusing array of thoughts and questions. He figured if he could understand it, then he could move on with his life. Leave her behind.

Isn't that what he wanted?

"How did you know it was true love?" He held up a hand in defense. "I don't mean that to be rude. To question your love for your—" he couldn't say husband "—for James. But how did you know what you felt for him wasn't lust? Wasn't something besides love?"

For a long while she didn't speak. He watched the muscles in her throat work up and down as she fought some battle within. With a shaky hand, she smoothed her hair back, making fine, golden strands sparkle in the sunlight that slanted through the windshield.

"I really don't want to... I can't discuss this with you. It's too painful."

Regret gripped him. In that moment he realized that his need, his longing had never gone away. It was buried inside him, smothered, but still alive, beating, striving for daylight. "Right. I understand."

It had been impossible for him to discuss his own heartache over Jillian when she'd bailed out of Winslow. She'd loved James. Still did. And she'd never loved Brody. Never would.

Five

You didn't lie, Jillian.

But she hadn't told the truth, either. Not exactly.

She closed her car door, already exhausted from the drive that had felt much longer than it actually took. The home and winery sat squarely on a prime piece of real estate that bordered the north side of the Fortunes' Double Crown Ranch. Taking a slow, calming breath, she absorbed the clean Indian-summer air, the warm breeze, the scent of gardenias.

Let Brody think you loved James. Then maybe he'll give you the space and peace you need.

"What d'you think?" Brody asked, meeting her at the hood of her Camry and facing the home in front of them.

It looked as perfect as a well-loved dollhouse. Hot-pink bougainvillea garnished the pristine white picket fence that skirted the sun-yellow clapboard house. Wedgwood-blue trim fringed the roof, windows and porch. Two wicker rockers welcomed guests at the front door. Ethereal blue flowers overflowed the window boxes like miniature waterfalls.

"It's not what I expected," she said, falling into step with him on the gravel path and heading toward the house.

"And what was that?" he asked.

She kept her gaze on the path, away from Brody. But she couldn't miss the way the sunlight shone on his black hair, catching in the slight waves. "Oh, I don't know," she said, trying to sound casual when her heart beat chaotically. "Something from the nineteenth century maybe. Not dilapidated, just patriarchal." She altered her voice to sound arrogant. "Pretentious, if you know what I mean. You know, wine barrels, snifters and cigars. Musty."

He laughed, the sound full of life, pulling her gaze back to him. His smile shot frissons of heat through her.

"You're in for a pleasant surprise, then," he said. "Come on." Putting his hand at the small of her back, he guided her up the steps, past the fragrant gardenia bushes.

Her nerve endings, electrified by his touch, reaffirmed her reasons for misleading him when she'd said it was too painful to discuss her marriage to James.

She'd suddenly realized that Brody's betrayal of her love was infinitely more painful and heartbreaking than all she'd endured with James. It didn't seem right, but it was true. Anger and frustration tormented her. She couldn't turn off her attraction to Brody. Nor could she deny the old fears and longings stirring inside her once more. Heaven help her!

"We have eighty acres under crop production." Ellie Shelton spoke with short, clipped diction as she squinted against the setting sun at the rows of vines carefully fastened to wood and wire trellises that crisscrossed the land.

The brilliant hues of evening shone on her faded red hair, which held more gray strands than what had once been vivid auburn. Pride as well as age lined Ellie's face.

Together the Sheltons had built their dream. And they faced their future hand in hand. Strange, perplexing emotions welled in Jillian's chest. She could barely concentrate on the discussion to take notes for Brody. Envy saturated every fiber of her being. She wondered what it would be like to grow old with someone, to know their thoughts as well as her own.

She'd wanted a marriage built on mutual respect and formidable love. It was her own fault that her dreams had crumbled. She should never have married James Tanner. She should have waited for the right man.

For Brody.

No! He was not the man for her. He had betrayed her when she'd been most vulnerable—when she'd opened her heart and exposed her soul. Obviously he hadn't cared, hadn't treasured her or their relationship the way she had. It had been just another acquisition, another conquest to him. Just as his business deals were now. At least he hadn't won—they hadn't made love. And she'd learned a valuable lesson—she'd never put herself in that position again.

She wanted a man to cherish her. If she wanted one at all.

"Let's get on to the wine cellar, Ellie." Deke Shelton tugged on his wife's hand. His smile lines creased his sun-tanned face. Despite his wavy silver hair that glinted in the waning sunlight, he looked like an eager little boy.

"In time." Ellie held her ground. "If Mr. Fortune is considering our property, he needs to know how our operation works. We can sample our wines later."

Jillian tensed. She'd thought they would only look over the property. She didn't think she'd be asked to sample wines. Being pregnant, she knew there was no way. But how would she explain her abstention? Her stomach lurched with sudden nerves.

Oblivious to her troubles, Brody studied the fields laid out in front of them. He crossed his arms over his broad chest. A tick in his jaw alerted Jillian to the tension mounting inside him. What had him so concerned?

"Ah, Ellie," Deke pouted, "that's the best part."

"Then we'll save the best for last." Lovingly, she patted her husband's arm. "You'll survive until then."

"I don't know," he muttered.

"You've stuck to the traditional French vines, have you not?" Brody asked.

"We've got a tasty little Pinot Noir." Deke rocked back and forth from heel to toe.

"The Pinot Noir and Chardonnay grow best in our limestone soil," Ellie explained. "We have twenty-five acres of Chardonnay, thirty of the Pinot—"

"It's my favorite." Deke grinned. "What's your preference, little lady?"

All eyes turned toward Jillian. Her spine stiffened. Her stomach flip-flopped. What could she say? "Uh, I'm really not sure, Mr. Shelton."

"Call me Deke. No need for formalities." He clapped Brody on the back. "Looks like we better hurry to the tasting room. We've got to show your assistant here the glories of wine.''

Jillian felt Brody's gaze on her. Her nerves bristled. How could she refuse to taste the Sheltons's wine without insulting them? More importantly, without explaining she was pregnant?

Maybe she was being silly, not telling Brody. After having worked for him for two weeks she doubted he would send her back to the secretarial pool.

Like a flash of lightning she remembered his soul-shattering kiss he'd given her. Correction. She'd helped make it a thorough kiss. She'd participated. She was equally at fault. Definite interest had sparkled in his hot gazes since, and part of her had gloried in that knowledge. She wanted him to want her, as a man wants a woman. As she had wanted him so long ago…as she wanted him now.

Another part of her had tried to deny it, tried to put barriers between them. None of her reactions made sense. Brody simply made her feel off balance. Maybe she should use her pregnancy to put one more barrier between them, a final one. Surely he'd lose interest in her quickly if he knew she was carrying another man's baby.

But the part of her that encouraged, needed, wanted Brody's interest balked at the idea of telling him. Not yet. Not now.

"This way, Brody, Jillian." Ellie gestured toward the back stairs that led down to a wooden deck and several footpaths arrowing toward the fields. "We'll show you the difference between a red grape and a white."

"We'll need to wet our whistle after standing out

in this heat for too long, Ellie,'' Deke complained, already wiping at beads of sweat dotting his forehead.

"Very well, then,'' his wife said, linking her arm with his. "We'll visit the tasting room after this. I've made you wait long enough.''

Jillian swallowed hard. She didn't have long to figure out her strategy.

"Here, taste it.'' Ellie offered Brody a plump grape right off the vine as they stood in the middle of a field, soft mounds of dirt beneath their feet. "It's all in the fruit.''

He hesitated, the grape rolling across his palm.

"Don't worry, Fortune. We don't use pesticides.'' Deke popped one into his mouth and chewed. He rolled his eyes as if in ecstasy. "Organically grown wine.''

"No worries, then.'' Testing it for himself, Brody tossed the grape into his mouth. A rich, vibrant flavor burst across his tongue. "Delicious.''

"You don't have a big vat where women stomp the grapes like in that 'I Love Lucy' episode, do you?'' Jillian asked.

"No, we don't,'' Ellie answered, pursing her lips. "We have presses that accomplish that nowadays.''

Deke laughed. "But that's a damn good idea, young lady.''

Jillie's rosy complexion brightened to the hue of strawberry wine, intoxicating Brody like he was seventeen.

"This way,'' Ellie stated, turning east and walking between rows of vines toward a limestone building with bold cedar beams, "to our tasting room. Sometimes we rent it out for weddings or receptions. It's centered above the wine cellar. After we allow Deke a few indulgences, we'll go below and see how we take the grapes and make the wine. It's quite a fascinating endeavor…'' Her voice drifted as the Sheltons walked hand in hand toward the large building along the edge of the field.

Brody fell further behind as he turned and waited for Jillian to catch up to him. She diverted her gaze, pretending to study a vine, her hand cupping a bunch of grapes, tenderly, carefully. He remembered her hands exploring his chest, clasping his back, stroking his jaw. Heat throbbed inside him.

He leaned close to her, breathing in her soft fragrance that reminded him of sailing in a sea of lilies. ''I'd been wondering the same thing.''

She jumped at his voice. Her turquoise eyes met his, alarm making them wide. ''What?''

''About how the grapes are pressed. You know, your comment about that 'I Love Lucy' episode.''

''Oh.'' She gave him a tentative smile. ''I don't think Mrs. Shelton appreciated my question.''

''Or the humor.'' He laughed. ''No worries about her. Remember watching that show together in college?''

She nodded but said nothing.

Together, they'd shared a bottle of wine and nibbled on grapes, taking sips each time Lucy said, ''Ricky!'' Mostly, they'd laughed and kissed. Old memories brought a surge of emotions that he'd forgotten—or ignored—for a long while. He could feel the heat of the sun on his shoulders, across the back of his neck. But the warmth he was experiencing was purely from Jillian's smile, the light in her blue-green eyes.

Bending, he plucked another Chardonnay variety from the vine and offered her a taste, pressing the plump fruit against her full bottom lip, as he had when they'd been almost lovers. ''What do you think, Jillie?''

The shock in her eyes alerted him that this was a different time, a different place. And Jillie certainly wasn't the woman he'd once known and loved. *What the hell are you doing?*

His temperature rose to match the late summer heat. Ever since she'd walked into the boardroom two weeks ago, he hadn't been able to stop thinking about her, those startling eyes, her warm, understanding smile, her intoxicating fragrance. That damn kiss. He hadn't been able to think straight since. He wasn't a teen anymore. This wasn't college. And he wasn't the same man he'd once been.

You fool! It hadn't simply been the last few weeks. It had been a problem for him for the past ten years. He'd never successfully vanquished Jillie from his mind...or his heart.

Standing as awkwardly as if he'd been caught buck-naked, offering her a tender grape, he waited for her response. The standoff lasted only a few seconds, but seemed an eternity in his mind. What if she turned away? Would she once again reject him? But what if she took the grape into her mouth? His throat went dry at the prospect.

Finally, arching her neck away from him, she stepped back and grabbed the grape with her hand.

Disappointment that she hadn't touched her mouth to his fingers twisted inside him.

Then he noticed a droplet of juice glistening in the sunlight on her bottom lip. Without hesitation, he brushed his thumb along her lip. His gut contracted with raw need.

Jillian looked suddenly pale, shaken. He felt the tremors rock through him. Concern twisted around his spine. What had he done?

"Are you all right?" he asked, his voice hoarse.

"I think we should go inside." She stepped farther away from him, pacing herself to catch up to the Sheltons who had disappeared inside the building.

He strode behind her and put a hand on her elbow, halting her escape when they reached the door. Her eyes widened and she flinched. "What's wrong?"

She pulled away, limping. "There's a rock in my sandal." Grabbing on to the door handle, she lifted her foot and slipped off her sandal. Before she could brush the bottom of her foot, he did it for her, smoothing his palm down the arch. A pebble fell to the ground. His throat cinched shut. When would he learn his lesson and avoid touching her?

"Are you all right now?"

She met his gaze squarely, but shuttered her emotions. "Y-yes. I'm fine."

He felt her tremble like a fragile leaf in a rain shower. "You don't look so fine."

"It's warm out here."

Nodding, he opened the door to the tasting room. It was damn hot, but the weather had nothing to do with the heat generated inside him.

He had to blink several times for his eyes to adjust

to the darkness inside the room. Forest-green paint covered the walls, giving the room an intimate feeling, even though it was as spacious as a ballroom with ceilings two stories high. Half-ton French oak barrels lined the walls from floor to ceiling. At the far end of the room was an extraordinary stone fireplace. Ellie knelt in front of it, twisting the gas starter. In front of the hearth, oak tables and leather chairs provided wine drinkers a place to kick back and indulge. Brody urged Jillian toward one of the comfortable seats.

At the sound of their steps on the stone floor, Ellie turned from the fireplace. "It doesn't put out much heat," she said, giving a nod to the gigantic ceiling fans spinning overhead. "It's mainly just for show. To give the room a cozier atmosphere." As her gaze settled on Jillian, she frowned. "Are you all right?"

"She got too hot outside," Brody answered, knowing he'd felt the intense heat, as well. But not from the sun. From Jillian. His attraction to her was like an overactive furnace in winter. "Could she have a glass of water?"

"Of course. It is warm outside. It's the time of year." Ellie rubbed her hands on the back of her jeans. "Deke went to find the perfect bottle of wine for us. But I'll get us all some water." Ellie headed toward the stairs that led to the cellar. "Brody, if you'd like, you could come down and Deke will start to show you the presses and such."

"I better stay here with Jillie. I can take a look later."

"Very well." She waved over her shoulder. "I'll be back in a jiffy."

After she left, the only sound in the room besides

the whirring of the ceiling fans and crackle of the fire was Jillian's shallow breathing. Worried, he watched her slide a yellow lolly into her mouth.

"Low blood sugar again?" he asked.

She nodded. "Uh, yes. But I'm feeling much better already. You don't have to baby-sit me. I'm okay. Why don't you go on and meet up with the Sheltons?"

"Because I'd rather be here. With you."

When her gaze collided with his, a spark erupted between them. He knew then his words were true, not just because of his concern for her health. But because he cared about Jillie. He cared too much.

"Brody—"

"This is a nice place," he said, interrupting her, charging forward like a bull. He couldn't stand the idea that she would rebuke him for caring. He didn't want her to put more distance between them. Plopping his suddenly tired body into a chair opposite Jillie's he looked around the vast room. It was a humbling place, making him feel small yet secure at the same time. Maybe it was Jillie that made him feel so damn vulnerable.

His gaze settled on a far window that looked out over the acres of vines and wide-stretching sky. The rugged land with its rocks and stubborn brush reminded him of home. He missed Australia, but seeing this place made him think he could stay here in America for the rest of his life. Studying the hard, stony land gave him a sense of freedom. Being with Jillie gave him a sense of home, a piece of hope.

"I could settle down somewhere like this." Surprised that he'd spoken his feelings out loud, he felt his muscles tense.

"You want a quiet life on a farm?" Incredulity filled her voice and eyes.

"You forget I was raised on a ranch."

"What about working for the Fortune dynasty?"

He shrugged, uncomfortable laying his plans out on the proverbial table, especially plans he wasn't sure of yet. "I'll always work for Fortune, TX, Ltd. It's my life, my family. That's the one thing you never understood about me," he said, remembering their discussions of family back in college. "I love my family. We're all very close, very supportive of one another."

For the first time he let his thoughts and feelings bubble to the surface. It gave him a sensation of freedom without regret or remorse. "I'm not a cattleman like my uncle. Or a horse breeder like my father. Never have been. I'm a businessman," he stated. "It's what I'm good at. What I love. But I can't deny who I am, where I came from, the love I feel for solid ground, my land, under my feet.

"I've been longing for a place to settle." He raked his fingers through his hair.

Her eyes were full and round. Firelight reflected in their depths giving them a rich, jewel-like quality.

Uneasy with sharing so much, he crossed his arms over his chest as if he could cover and protect himself from the pain of exposure.

"I understand more than you think. Back in college, I was close to my mother. But I couldn't get past the fact that my father had left, that I didn't really have a family, a home. But I understand more now.

I always had a real family. It was just different from yours. Ever since Mom died, I've been searching…needing my family. You're very lucky, Brody, to have yours."

Something in her tone startled him, made him sense she truly understood. He narrowed his gaze on her. He wanted to believe she could understand him. At the same time it scared him how much it mattered. How much *she* mattered.

"I am," he said solemnly, truthfully.

Sliding the lolly across her tongue and unknowingly melting his insides in that same instant, she said, "I do have my sister. We're much closer than we used to be. She's why I moved to San Antonio after James died. So I understand your love of family, maybe better…now that I've lost so much."

"Maybe we have more in common now than we used to." Tightness coiled inside him. "You always knew me so well."

She shook her head. "No. I thought I did. But I'm not sure anybody truly knows another person."

His spine stiffened. Apprehension strangled the hope that had grown. "What does that mean?"

She looked away. "Oh, Brody—"

Without the warmth of her gaze, a chill blew through him like a wintry breeze. "You had it right when you said I'd lived a life on easy street. I didn't know heartache or suffering."

She tilted her head, her gaze slanting toward him. "When did I say that?"

His insides twitched with nervous energy. Why did he always have to test the boundaries of their relationship?

"Years ago," he stated carefully, concealing more than he revealed. "When we were in school."

He remembered when they'd first become friends, before their friendship had blossomed into love. She'd considered him a carousing playboy and hadn't held her tongue. He'd respected her for her honesty. And he'd set out to prove her wrong.

"September twenty-ninth, our sophomore year, to be exact." The date—the moment—was branded on his memory. "We were walking across campus. It had started to rain."

"You remember what I said back then?"

"I remember everything." He leaned forward, his chest tight. "You were the first person to tell me the truth, to speak your mind. Besides my family. You were fearless. You didn't have a hidden agenda and I respected you for that. Still do. Most women don't bother, are afraid my ego can't take it, or are more worried about how the consequences of the truth will affect them. Most people want something from me."

He stopped himself from going further. Had he said too much? Hell, he was crowing like a kookaburra. Trying to read her thoughts, he was surprised when her mouth curved into a soft, intoxicating smile. Maybe he hadn't overplayed his hand. "I've changed, you know."

"We've all changed." She shifted in her seat, crossing her legs, trying to avoid his intense gaze, his closeness, as if trying to put a barrier between them. "So you think now you've experienced heartache and despair...like real people?"

"You make me sound like a spoiled child."

"Brody, I meant—"

He waved his hand to silence her protest. "It's all right. I was spoiled. Hell, I had everything I'd ever wanted. A caring family. A nice home. Money. Cars."

"Women," she said with a subtle smile.

"Maybe." But not the one he'd wanted. "I had it damn easy." Until...

"And now you think you need to suffer?"

He chuckled at the absurdity of this situation. "I've already done that."

A line creased her forehead, dragging her eyebrows down into a concerned frown. "What happened?"

Her interest touched him. Could she...did she care?

He settled back into the warmth of the leather chair and folded his hands over the armrests. Remembering the pain of Jillie leaving him, he tightened his grip. He never wanted to forget that feeling. Remembering would prevent him from experiencing the fear, anger and heartache again.

"I learned I can't have everything." His voice resonated with the truth. "But I don't mind working or fighting for what I really, truly want."

And he really, truly wanted Jillie.

Determination surged inside him, fortifying him. Maybe he could have all he'd ever wanted. Maybe it would just take time and a lot of patience.

Maybe she needed time to get over James. Just as he needed time to adjust to the idea of finding her again.

When Jillie reached over and put her hand on his arm, his muscles jumped with surprise, his heart jolted with excitement. The soft glow in her eyes warmed his soul. "I believe you'll get whatever it is you want."

In that moment, gazing into her blue-green eyes, he started to believe it might be possible, too.

"What do you want out of life now, Jillie?" he asked, his rugged accent drawing her into a safe cocoon, making her forget the Sheltons downstairs, her surroundings, her reasons for keeping an emotional shield between her and Brody.

She leaned back in her chair, closed her eyes briefly and breathed deeply. For the first time since she'd seen Brody again, she felt calmer in his presence.

When she looked back at him, his gray eyes were full of understanding and acceptance. The part of her heart that had been closed off, protected for so long, began to open.

Knowing her heart, she answered truthfully. "I want a place to call home."

"You never really had that, did you?" Empathy saturated his words. She sensed no condemnation, no pity.

"Not the kind you had. Since I grew up without a father, I think for a long time I was searching for…" She stopped herself. What was she about to reveal? That she'd married James, hoping for the security she'd never felt? She shifted in her chair, sucked on the tart lemon candy in her mouth. She shouldn't feel this comfortable with Brody. She had to keep up her guard.

"Searching for what?" His voice lured her to share with him all her feelings, all her anguish, all her fears.

Resisting, she squared her shoulders against the need to lean on him. "A real home."

"And now you've lost it again." His gaze was as soft as a billowing cloud.

She wanted to rest in his gentle understanding. Suddenly she felt exhausted, fatigue settled into her bones. He stirred old feelings inside her, longings that she'd relinquished years ago. He made her want to hope again. And that frightened her.

She'd never had a real home as a kid. Or as a married woman. Her mother had tried, wearing herself out to provide her girls with everything she thought they deserved. James, with his lucrative banking job in Amarillo and his daddy's help, had bought a beautiful house, but she'd quickly learned that a home was more than brick and mortar, custom drapes and a Jacuzzi tub. She'd wanted, needed, yearned for more. Something she'd quickly realized James couldn't give—love.

"You can't lose something you never had," she answered, feeling a strength she hadn't known existed emerge like a phoenix inside her. Her baby. The words resonated in her head. *Her* baby was a gift. Maybe it was all the family, the only home, she would ever have, ever need.

But she couldn't explain her heart to Brody. Knowing a tiny baby was nestled safe inside her along with her hopes and desires, she stated with firm conviction, "I haven't lost everything."

His steel gaze penetrated her soul. "What's that mean?"

Feeling too vulnerable, she looked into the flames guarded by the stone fireplace. Much like the controlled fire, she felt her dreams blaze inside her, burning her soul, blackening her spirit when the flames were unable to penetrate the walls she'd placed around them.

She couldn't tell Brody the truth. But she couldn't deny her desires to herself. She wanted, needed, yearned for someone to love her, to cherish her. But that was a fairy tale wish. What she desired even more was for a gentle, loving man to be a father to her baby. She knew all too well what it was like to grow up without a father, without a complete family.

Muffled footsteps provided relief from the intimacy she resisted sharing with Brody. She refused to care about him the way she once had. She didn't need him. Didn't want him.

That, she realized, was a bold lie.

"Sorry it took me so long," Ellie interrupted, carrying a tray of water glasses and wine goblets.

"It's my fault," Deke said, coming up the stairs behind his wife. Their voices carried through the cavernous room. "We had a disagreement over which wine we should sample. So I brought a couple of bottles."

"He wanted you to try one of our Merlots from a few years back. It is a good vintage. But with the heat, I thought a crisp Chardonnay would be better."

Deke studied one of the chilled bottles. "It has sold well." Applying the corkscrew to the top, he opened the bottle and sighed with pleasure when the cork pulled free. "Not a better sound in the world."

Grinning, he poured wine into the goblets that Ellie had placed on the round table. Then he handed a glass of golden wine to each of them.

Unsure what to do, Jillian waited until Brody made a toast.

"To good wine—" his gaze sought hers "—and vintage friendships."

Her heart contracted. He was right. He had changed. For the better. Or maybe the worse. He made her want to love him again. And she couldn't—wouldn't—make that mistake twice.

Taking his cue, she pressed the cool edge of the goblet against her lips and pretended to taste the wine.

"What do you think?" Deke asked.

"Very refreshing," Brody answered, sipping more of the Chardonnay.

Deke and Ellie looked toward Jillian. She muttered an appropriate response. But they didn't seem satisfied.

Frowning, Deke insisted. "Try it again. I bet by the time you finish that glass you'll be feeling much better."

Her insides turned cold. She couldn't continue the charade any further. She didn't have a choice. Carefully, she set the goblet on the table. "I'm sorry, but I don't drink."

Brody's startled gaze pinned her. She knew he remembered sharing bottles of wine during television shows and over candlelight dinners. She recognized the changes in him as easily as she saw the lines pinching the corners of his mouth. But obviously he didn't understand that she'd changed, too.

She knew when they were alone again she'd have to explain. Now what would she say?

Six

"You don't feel well," Brody stated, walking toward Jillian's car after thanking the Sheltons for their hospitality and tour of their property. "I'll drive."

At Jillie's startled look, he explained, "I have my international license. I'll be careful with your Yank tank."

He'd anticipated an argument, but she handed him the keys and with a tired sigh climbed into the passenger seat. Concern clouded his thoughts. In college Jillian had always been energetic. Now she had about as much energy as the pumpkin patch he drove past. Was something wrong? Was she ill? Maybe he was being overly protective.

But then he remembered her clipped statement that she didn't drink. Since when?

He drove a couple of miles down the highway, his gaze on the road that extended into the darkness beyond, his hands gripping the steering wheel.

"Is something wrong?" she asked. "You look as if you're going to strangle that steering wheel."

"Yeah, I'd say so." He cut to the chase of his irritation, ignoring his concern for her constant exhaustion. It was probably because she didn't eat breakfast unless he brought her a bagel. Which he now did every day. Irritation was simpler than admitting he really cared about her. "Why did you insult our hosts by refusing to drink their wine?"

She took a deep breath and leaned back into the seat, tilting her head against the headrest and closing her eyes. Slowly, she released a pent-up breath. "Because my husband died in a drunk driving accident."

Guilt ripped through him, tore apart his petty anger. And he'd been worried about her tasting a damn bottle of wine!

"Why didn't you tell me? I wouldn't have asked you to come today."

"It's all right, Brody." She sounded weary. Lifting her hand, she let it fall back to her lap, limp, tired. "It doesn't matter."

"It does. It matters a lot. I shouldn't have put that kind of pressure on you. I'm sorry—"

"I'm okay, Brody." A slight edge entered her voice. "Forget it."

But he couldn't.

A couple of miles passed with nothing but silence between them. He glanced at her twice—okay, three times. Her skin looked pale, almost translucent in the moonlight. Her mouth had compressed into a thin line. From aggravation? Anger? Grief? Illness?

"Brody," she said, her voice tentative, "I owe you an apology."

Confused, he shot her a glance then jerked his attention back to the roadway. "No worries, Jillie. I understand your reasons. If anybody owes anyone an apology, it's me. I didn't mean to upset you, to remind you—"

"You don't owe me anything." Her voice sounded solid, firm, full of conviction. "I'm not upset." But she ground each word between her teeth as if trying to gain control.

"You're not?"

She shook her head. "Numb, maybe. I haven't felt anything for a long time." She spoke carefully, uttering each word as if stepping gingerly over rocky terrain. "I—I misled you. And I was wrong."

"About what?" he prodded, confused by her statement.

Another heavy sigh, this one was filled with exhaustion. "James was drunk the night he died. He caused the wreck. Took his own life." She swallowed hard. "And the lives of two others."

Her statement shot through him like a bullet. Stunned, he felt his body tremble, a shudder of outrage, revulsion, denial. He had to force himself to watch the road. What had Jillian been through the last few months...or years? What had James done to her?

He cursed James. The bloody fool. *I was right. Goddamn it, I was right! James was no damn good.*

The knowledge brought no satisfaction, only a deep resonating sorrow. Brody had always believed the man Jillian had married was worthless, a bum. But he'd convinced himself his convictions were based on jealousy and not justified. After all, he'd had no proof. He'd never met James.

An oppressive weight descended on Brody's shoulders. It was his fault. He should have stopped Jillian from marrying James. He should have gone after her when she left Winslow. He should have done something...anything to protect her. But the simple truth was she might have chosen James over him, anyway. The realization burned in his gut.

Jillie's head fell forward, her shoulders slumped. Silent, shoulder-shaking tears splashed against the backs of her hands, which she clasped tightly in her lap. Her pain saturated his soul, flooded his senses. Regret pounded against him in violent waves.

Cautiously, he maneuvered the car into the far right lane and searched for a chance to pull over. At the first opportunity, he jerked the steering wheel and swerved into a parking lot. Tires crunched gravel. He drove to a far corner and stopped under the protection of an oak tree away from the security lights...away from any curious gazes.

"Jillie..." When he turned toward her, his heart contracted. He locked the blame on himself. He should have done something. He would do something now to help her. But what?

His insides shifted uncomfortably. What if she cried for James? Not for the heartache he'd caused? Uncertainty gripped his stomach. He ran his hands down the creases of his jeans. Unsure what to do, shaken by her tears, he remembered her words about how she'd felt numb for a long time. Maybe all he could do now was let her cry. Be there for her to lean on.

But he felt utterly helpless.

"Ah, Jillie," he said, unable to sit by and watch her suffer alone. He pulled her into his arms, cradling her head against his shoulder, wrapping his arms around her slight form. Her trembling shook him to the core. He absorbed each tremor and soaked up her tears with his shirt.

Her hoarse cries reverberated in his head, made his ears ache, his heart bleed. Her anguish penetrated the deepest recesses, skewered him as nothing else had ever done. His arms tightened around her as he tried to contain his own anger and regret, tried to absorb her pain into him.

Her fingers pressed into his back, digging, clawing with need. He rocked her from side to side as he would a small child. But he felt only what a man feels for a woman, strong, powerful compassion. She was a survivor. And she'd get through this. He'd make sure of it.

The moments passed quietly as her tears began to slow. Darkness shrouded them in secrecy, guarding, protecting, uniting them together. Her shudders ebbed, becoming less intense, less frequent until she relaxed against him, spent and exhausted. She sniffled against his shirtfront. He smoothed his hands along her back, molding her to him, offering what he knew words couldn't.

"I'm sorry." His chest muffled her voice but the words struck his heart. "I didn't mean to break down."

"No reason to be sorry." His fingers traced the column of her spine over and over. He never wanted to let her go.

That realization stunned him. It shouldn't. A part of him had known that his love for Jillian had never died. But fear spiked inside him. What if she didn't need him? What if she ran away from him again?

In that moment he secured a barrier around his heart. He had to wait to see what Jillie wanted, what she needed, who she loved. If it was still James, Brody knew he'd have to walk away.

"I haven't spoken of...of his accident...

James's..." She shrugged as if uncomfortable even saying her husband's name. He wondered if it was because of her love. Or grief. "T-to anyone."

"Then it's time."

Again she sniffled. Knowing the moment was slipping away, he shifted, reaching for his back pocket, and handed her his handkerchief.

"Thank you." She gave him a soft, embarrassed smile.

He had an overwhelming urge to lift her face, blot away her tears with the soft cotton and kiss her until she couldn't remember or care about the past, until she could only cling to him in utter surrender. Until her numbness turned to passion. But he resisted, sensing it was too soon. Too many questions needed to be answered. She needed a moment to compose herself. She needed time to heal. He needed to know her heart first.

"I've really embarrassed myself now, haven't I?" She tried an awkward laugh.

"I wouldn't say that. You've been through a lot."

She nodded. "More than you know."

He wanted to say "Tell me," but he swallowed the words. He waited, using more patience than he knew he owned. It had to be when she was ready.

She took a deep, shuddering breath, as if releasing the rest of the tension inside her. "I guess you've figured out I...James and I had a less than perfect marriage."

His jaw clenched. "Didn't know there was such a thing."

"Maybe you're right." She shrugged. "I'm definitely not an expert on the subject. But ours was even below normal standards.''

She brushed her hair back from her face. ''I knew from the first day...maybe even before...that I'd made a mistake. But I was determined to make it work. I can be stubborn.''

''Right.'' He chuckled, remembering her tenacity, her strength of conviction when they'd argued, her determination when she'd studied for a difficult exam. He'd admired her ability to persevere and bulldoze her way into college. ''It was always the part I admired most about you.''

Her gaze lifted to meet his. Her eyes were deep and full and surging like the ocean, unsure, tortured, wild. Damn. He'd said too much, spoken out of turn. When she looked back at her hands, twisting the handkerchief between her fingers, he felt a cold shudder rock him.

''It was always one-sided,'' she continued, ignoring his comment. ''James never worked to save our marriage. Probably never even thought it was in danger.

''He had what he wanted. A proper wife. And he wanted to continue enjoying himself, as he had when he was single. He didn't think anything should change once we said our vows.'' Her voice choked. ''I guess they meant more to me than to him.''

Brody kept her tucked safely under his arm but remained silent, listening, waiting.

''James liked to drink,'' she said matter of factly. ''Liked to go out with the boys. And he did. Almost every night. Oh, most of the time he said it was for business. But I knew better. I heard rumors. I knew how much he drank.

"He figured he could get away with it. His daddy wasn't going to fire him from the bank. And I wasn't going to leave."

"Why not?" Brody cursed himself for asking. But he couldn't imagine why she'd want to stay.

"Because I believed…still believe in marriage. I wanted to be true to my vows."

Rage imploded inside Brody. He had nowhere to aim his anger, nowhere to release it. "Even if he wasn't true to his?"

"Yes." Her lips pressed into a tight line. "At least he hadn't left. Like my daddy left my momma when I was a little girl. Just walked out and never looked back." Her hands folded into fists. "I wasn't going to be like him. And I wasn't going to let James be like that, either. We'd made a commitment. No one forced me to say 'I do.' I made the decision to marry James with a clear head. I knew what he was like…sort of…but not completely. And I was going to stick to it. No matter what."

Silence reverberated in the confines of the car. Brody's ears roared as blood pounded in his temples. Her words proved what he'd always known. She'd chosen James. Of her own free will. The knowledge hit him like a sledgehammer to his heart. But had her love for James died even before he'd met his death?

"Do you remember calling me a few months ago?" She laughed. It was a stark, incredulous sound. "God, what a shock. Over the years, when it had been almost impossible to stay with James, not to just walk out, I'd dreamed of you calling me. Of you sensing something was wrong. Of you coming to the States and rescuing me from my marriage. Ridiculous, huh?''

He shook his head, unable to speak as a ball of hard emotions jammed his throat. And he'd dreamed she'd returned to him. Both had been too proud. He wished now that he had gone after her. If only he'd known. If only he hadn't been so self-absorbed with his own anger. If only he'd taken a chance, followed his gut instinct.

"James and I had a terrible argument…that night you called. A real whopper. He stormed out and I knew he wouldn't be home until morning. Then he would stagger in drunk.

"I think by then I was starting to suspect he was seeing another woman…" She arched an eyebrow. "Maybe I should say—other women. But I didn't want to believe it. Oh, I'd heard the rumors. But I'd ignored them. Nothing was going to destroy my marriage. So, I turned a deaf ear. I sent his clothes to the cleaner's so I wouldn't catch a whiff of perfume or find lipstick stains or phone numbers scribbled on napkins.

"James had his faults. No one would deny he liked his Scotch. A little too much. But I couldn't believe he'd…" She swallowed hard, as if still trying to accept it. "I didn't want to believe or know he'd do that."

"Why not?" Brody asked, finding his voice at last. He believed James was a jerk and he'd never met the bloke.

"Because then I could live with myself, with my choices, my mistakes. James and I had known each other since we were eight years old. We'd grown up together, gone to school together every day since second grade. We'd been high school sweethearts. I just couldn't believe he would do what y—" Her spine stiffened and she moved away from Brody, scooting back into the passenger seat. "I refused to believe it, that's all."

Brody's arms felt cold, his heart empty.

"Anyway—" she sniffed and squared her shoulders "—when you called that night a few months ago... I'd been feeling really alone. God, hearing your voice brought back so many memories. Good and bad. It reminded me of how empty my life was. How much had changed. How much I'd lost."

She took a deep breath before continuing. "I wanted to pour out my heart to you. I wanted to ask for your help. I wanted...needed..." She tilted her head into her hands, then brushed her hair back and stared up at the roof of the car. "But I couldn't."

"Why?" If only she'd said something, given him a hint...anything!

She shrugged. "I was embarrassed, ashamed. Lots more reasons, I suppose. Most don't matter anymore."

"I would have done anything for you." The words were bold, true.

She looked at him then, her eyes hard and penetrating. "Would you?"

"If you'd understood that," he said, "you never would have left Australia."

A cold chill shuddered through Jillian. How could he say that? How could *he*, of all people, claim something like that? How could he have cared for her when he'd been seeing...sleeping with his old girlfriend Gail? Stark anger stripped away the rest of her emotions. She glared at Brody, sitting smugly across the seat from her. She wanted to blame him.

If he hadn't two-timed her, if he'd *really* loved her, then she wouldn't have felt so lost, so alone after her mother died. Maybe then she would have returned to Australia. Instead of marrying James.

But the truth resonated inside her, sapping her strength, her resolve, her anger. It was her fault. Hers alone. She was to blame for her own decisions. No one else. Not even James.

Since his death, she'd taken on the responsibility of her decisions. She wouldn't live with anger or regret. She'd left Brody. She'd married James. Now she had her own life to live...her baby to raise.

Then why did her heart still ache?

Because, she realized with shame, that she was more upset about Brody's indiscretion with Gail, than with all of her husband's cheating during their marriage. It's why she'd so easily ignored or denied the rumors about James.

Why? Was she loony? She hadn't married Brody, for God's sake! Her husband had broken his vows. Their wedding vows! Why didn't that make the ground beneath her feet crumble?

The answer was too easy, but all too true. Maybe she'd expected that kind of behavior from James. But not from Brody. She'd believed from the first day she'd met the tall, handsome Australian that he was honorable, trustworthy. He'd shown her in actions and deeds what words could never convey. Then her beliefs had been shaken when Gail had told her the truth. Everything she'd believed about Brody, all the trust she'd placed in him, had disintegrated.

Maybe that's why it had been easy to marry James. She hadn't expected much from him. She hadn't given of herself. Hadn't loved him desperately, urgently, passionately. The way she had Brody. That's why James's affairs and the tragedy of his death didn't touch her heart in the same way or break her into jagged pieces.

Oh, God! I didn't love James. I didn't love my husband. I didn't love the father of my baby.

Horrified at the new revelations spinning through her, she clenched her hands, her nails digging into her palms.

She hadn't allowed herself to love James. Because she'd loved Brody. And she'd hung on to that hopeless, foolish love even though he'd shattered her heart.

Distraught, she shifted her gaze beyond Brody, too mortified to meet his concerned gaze, too horrified by his power over her emotions. She stared out the driver's window toward a nearby Victorian-style house. Shadows encased it. The roof peaks pointed toward the starry sky.

Where had they stopped? In someone's driveway?

Embarrassment rose to her cheeks, burned her skin until it tingled. Then her gaze located a sign in the yard. Yarboroughs's Bed And Breakfast.

Her nerves electrified. "What are we doing here?"

He twisted his head, following her gaze. "Hmm. Maybe it's a sign we should spend the night."

Seven

"**I** don't think so," Jillian stated, her blue eyes searing Brody like twin laser beams, slicing, penetrating, burning.

He gave a full-bodied laugh. "I know what you're thinking."

She crossed her arms over her chest. "And what's that?"

"I'm not looking to ravage your body."

Shaking his head, he admitted that was exactly what he wanted to do. But he couldn't confess, because it hadn't been his reason for pulling into the B and B's parking lot. Maybe fate had dealt him a new hand.

"Look, it's late. We're both exhausted." He dragged his fingers through his hair, trying to make her understand. "If there had been a drive-in movie here, I would have paid the admission so we could have talked. If it had been a garbage dump, it would have worked just as well."

Her eyes softened around the edges. "That wouldn't have had the same effect."

Heat shot through him. Any setting would do for him. "Luckily it's a nice bed and breakfast." He shrugged casually, as if it mattered little whether it was a motel or a five-star inn. "We can rest here then drive back in the morning. No harm. Promise."

She slanted a worried glance in his direction. "How long till we could be home...I mean, back to San Antonio?"

"At least three hours. Maybe four."

She gave a heavy sigh, her shoulders slumping with fatigue. The faint lines at the corners of her eyes deepened. "You're probably tired, too. It wouldn't be fair to ask you to drive while I sleep."

"I would, if you asked." He'd do anything for her. But he wanted this extra time with her and he didn't want to analyze why.

Jutting out her chin, she asked, "Separate rooms?"

"Of course." It was too soon. She needed time. And he planned on giving her what she needed, no matter how much he wanted her in his bed. He also suspected he needed time, too.

"Well, maybe it would be for the best. No reason to hurry back, I suppose. Tomorrow is Sunday. And it's dangerous to drive when you're tired." As if resigning herself, she unfolded her arms. "All right. I'll give my sister a call and let her know."

"Good," Brody stated, suddenly rejuvenated. This overnight stay would give him the opportunity to spend more time with Jillian. That's all he wanted. "I'll get us a room—"

She skewered him with a look.

"Right. Two rooms," he corrected. "Then we can get some dinner. I'm starved." He was starved for more than food. But he could wait. He could wait an eternity. If he only knew there was a chance with Jillie.

* * *

''Brody Smith,'' he told the manager of the B and B, wrenching Jillian's attention away from the pamphlets advertising local tourist attractions.

Smith? Her brow wrinkled with confusion. Tiny hairs at the back of her neck stood poised.

The manager's suspicious gaze shifted toward her as he peered at her through his thick glasses. The man had grown his hair long on one side and combed it over the bald spot on top of his head.

Smith! Something exploded inside her. Her hand closed on the pamphlet she'd been examining, crushing it against her palm.

Who the heck was Brody *Smith?* Brody sounded as if he was arranging some tawdry rendezvous. Her nerves stretched to the breaking point. *He better be getting two separate rooms or he'll be sleeping in the car. Alone. Better yet, he'll be hitchhiking his way back to San Antonio.*

She glared at Brody's back, his broad, muscle-rounded shoulders. All too clearly, she remembered the strength, the security those shoulders had provided earlier. Her fingers had frantically traced the contours of his back, feeling the ridges of his spine, the smooth planes of muscle and sinew. An irritating heat surged inside her. She'd felt comforted, protected in his arms, guarded by his broad chest. And she'd felt a whole lot more. Titillating sensations she didn't want to examine too closely.

Bracing herself, she set aside those thoughts. Brody didn't want her. Not now. Not after the mess she'd made of her life. She hooked a curtain of hair behind one ear. Her imagination had gone off the deep end again.

Trying to smooth out the creases she'd caused in the pamphlet along with the crinkles along her nervous system, she knew deep in her heart that Brody wouldn't take advantage of this situation. If he'd been so inclined, then he could have made a pass at her in the car, when his arms were wrapped around her, when she'd been vulnerable, weak.

Or had he gotten the wrong impression then? And expected more now?

No, no, no. I made it clear. Didn't I? That there would be two separate bedrooms.

All she could remember at the moment was staring up into his flannel-gray eyes, feeling a tingle of warmth low in her abdomen. She'd wanted him to kiss her. To kiss her as he had only a few weeks ago. To kiss her the way he had ten years ago. She wanted his kiss, needed it like nourishment.

Tingles of anticipation rippled down her spine and settled in an agonizing pool of cold, knee-knocking fear. She wasn't sure which frightened her more, the way Brody had broken her heart in the past or the way he affected her now. Both made her heart palpitate. She felt somehow more vulnerable now. As if a rejection from him would be far more devastating.

Refusing to look closer at the answers hidden in her heart, she focused on the conversation between Brody and the B and B manager. Their words were low, murmured. Unable to understand their conversation, she felt her nerves bristle with apprehension. James and Brody had taught her well—not to trust.

What was Brody up to now?

With every ounce of restraint she could muster, she held back her questions. No use making a scene in

front of the poor, defenseless manager who looked as
though he'd been awakened while sleeping in front
of the television. But later…oh, later she'd question
the devil out of Brody Fortune.

A scant ten minutes later, Jillian found herself
seated across from Brody at a cherrywood table covered with a cutwork linen tablecloth. With hunger
pains gnawing at her belly, she was not in a position
to argue. Yet.

She twisted the starched napkin in her lap around
her fingers. The dining room was small, intimate and
made her feel like a klutz in a china shop. She felt
thick and awkward as she sat on the dainty chair. Age
creaked in the wooden joints, giving her an extra dose
of insecurity.

"Would you like to start with a bottle of wine?"
the B and B manager asked. "We buy our stock ex-
clusively from a local winery. There's a Merlot, a
very nice vintage."

"No, thanks, mate." Brody leaned back in his
chair. "What do you have on the menu this evening?"

Something irrational and romantic softened inside
Jillian at his dismissal of the manager's suggestion
for wine. She dipped her head, knowing why he'd
turned down the Merlot. Resisting the urge to thank
him, she remembered his private discussion with the
manager, his use of the name Smith. That successfully
put starch back in her spine.

"How about a couple of rib eyes? Scalloped potatoes and fresh asparagus?"

Brody glanced at her then. His eyes sparkled like

sun-drenched diamonds. "Is that all right with you, Jillie?"

She nodded, feeling her stomach rumble at the thought of food. Keeping her tone neutral, so as not to give away any of her contradictory feelings, she said, "Fine."

With a nod, the man scuttled around the table like a crab on the beach. He lit two white candles in the middle of the table and dimmed the lights of the chandelier, creating a romantic atmosphere that she wasn't prepared for. And didn't want.

When the deft little man left them alone to fetch glasses of water, she leaned toward Brody, clenching her hands as if they were clutching the cloth of his shirt, and whispered, "Why are you using the name Smith? If you're thinking that—"

"Reporters," he stated.

"What?" She sat back, stunned by his words.

"Uncle Ryan told us when we arrived in the States to be cautious. Reporters are always interested in the doings of the For—" He paused, glanced over his shoulder and then under the table as if he was under surveillance. "Never can be too careful." He gave her an infectious grin that melted her irritation. "Lately there's been even more publicity than any of us cares for. And Griff has us all paranoid about a maniac murderer on the loose."

"Who?" she asked, shocked by the news.

He shrugged his wide shoulders as if it wasn't anything she should be concerned with. "I was simply protecting your reputation. Or did you want to be mentioned in the local newspaper's society column?"

She shook her head. "N-no. No, thank you." She'd

been tied to enough headlines in Amarillo when James crashed his car. Tilting her head to the side, she asked, "Then you weren't...I mean, you didn't get just one room?"

"Two. As requested." He rested his elbows on the table, confident. Arrogant, she corrected. And too darn sexy for his own good. Or hers. "We'll have to share a dunny. Is that all right?"

Share a bathroom? Oh, heavens!

He gave her a smile that dissolved her resistance. "Ladies first, of course." The way his Australian tongue looped around the word "ladies" made her toes curl inside her sandals.

"I suppose we can manage." She smoothed her napkin across her lap.

Concern shot a hole through her cooperative spirit. Did that mean that their bedrooms were next to each other? Side by side? She'd feel as if she was sleeping in the same bed! She'd be within throwing distance of Brody as he slept, changed, showered. Her nerve endings sizzled.

The manager intruded, carrying a tray with two goblets and a crystal pitcher filled with water. "Can I get you an appetizer before your dinner is served? Maybe some Brie? Or garlic bread?"

Brody inclined his head toward Jillian, indicating it was her decision. "Brie would be nice," she answered.

With an approving smile, the manager disappeared back into the kitchen.

Candlelight flickered on the gold-flocked ruby wallpaper, creating shadows and shrinking the room around them. As dinner progressed, Brody charmed her with anecdotes and college stories. Jillian's nerves twisted into tedious knots. Brody was too charming. Too sexy. Too…much to resist.

She ate but barely tasted the steak and potatoes. Cognizant of her growing waistline, she skipped the Hollandaise sauce on the asparagus.

"Who else besides Griffin came over with you from Australia?" she asked, taking a sip of water. Ice tinkled against the crystal.

"Originally, my parents came to meet my father's long-lost brother, Ryan Fortune." His silverware clinked softly as he cut into his steak. "When Uncle Ryan and his new wife Lily visited us in New South Wales during their honeymoon trip, they invited us to come to San Antonio. Reed and I came over for business. Matilda came along for the ride. And Griff is guarding us all like a hawk."

"From anything or anyone specifically?"

"He's the cautious type."

"No one else came?" she asked, slanting her gaze toward the crystal salt and pepper shakers, too embarrassed to look him in the eye. She wondered about Gail. If their relationship was more than strictly business. An undercurrent of jealousy tugged at her.

"That's right." His eyes narrowed on her. "Is there someone you wish had?"

"N-no. Not at all. I was just curious." Readjusting her napkin, she changed the subject as quickly as possible. "How old is Matilda now? She must have been—what?—Eleven when I met her?"

"Right. She's twenty-one and constantly reminding us all she's an adult and free to do as she wishes."

He frowned and carved into his steak too enthusiastically. "She's about to give Griff and me gray hair."

"My sister says the same thing about me." She chuckled. "I guess that's what little sisters are for."

He shook his head in a disapproving way. "Makes me not ever want a daughter of my own. I don't think I could take it."

A cold slice of disappointment cut through her. She reached for her abdomen but stopped herself. She didn't know if she was having a girl or a boy. But Brody's words put one more barrier between them.

That was good. Right?

"Are you thinking of getting married?" She tried to sound casual, indifferent, but she couldn't deny the pounding of her heart as she waited for his answer. "You mentioned earlier that you wanted to settle down." Her voice squeaked. She remembered him speaking to that woman on the phone. Who was she? Some woman with an Aussie accent and sexy voice had called for Brody at the office a couple of times. But she'd never given her name. And Jillian had never had the nerve to ask if she was Gail. She was afraid she knew the answer already. "Is there some-one…a woman…"

His gaze leveled on her. "Thinking of one more and more."

Despair swelled over her. But wasn't this what she wanted? Brody married, unavailable? And far away from her? Yes, yes, of course.

"But only if I could have a marriage like my parents'," he added. "They have a true partnership. A love that defies explanation or hardship. I want a marriage that will last forever. I won't settle for anything less.''

The firm conviction in his voice made her own throat tighten. She'd wanted that, too. But she'd fallen so short. She'd never wanted her future children to be affected by a bad marriage the way she had been. Or to raise a child without a partner, a husband, a father for her child. That's exactly what would happen when she brought this baby into the world. A slow, burning anger raged inside her at the unfairness of it. But would it have been better if James were alive? She'd made choices…bad ones, but she'd give her child everything she could.

But could she give her baby a father? She doubted Brody would want to take on that kind of responsibility. He'd already practically said he didn't want kids! One more reason, she decided, he wouldn't be interested in her.

''Maybe that's what I was looking for,'' she said, thinking back to when she decided to marry James. ''Something opposite of what my parents had…that is, before my dad left us.'' She shoved away those painful memories. She couldn't dwell in the past. Not when she had the future of her baby to worry about. ''It's not easy creating a marriage like that. That kind of love, that kind of relationship, seems as rare as a perfect gem.''

''I'm willing to wait for that perfect lady.'' His eyes shone like marbles, solid, durable, unforgettable.

She wasn't perfect. And she wasn't the woman for Brody!

Hot piercing jealousy stabbed her heart. Was he thinking of Gail? ''It takes more than finding the right person. It takes commitment.'' She aimed the next blow at James's memory and directly at Brody's conscience. "It takes fidelity. Responsibility. Trust.''

Unflinching, he met her gaze as if he had no guilt whatsoever. "I'm not James.''

No, she thought, you're Brody. The damage he'd caused had cut her deeper, caused more scars. Because she'd truly loved him.

But was he really so callous as to not care or be aware of the hurt he'd caused? Or had he changed? Really changed. Could a man transform himself that much? Or was the fabric a man was made of constant and durable, only the cut and stitching variable over time?

Finally she asked herself the starkest question, the one that struck at the heart of her concerns. Could she ever trust Brody again? With her love? With her baby's?

Her answer made her more nervous, more agitated, more afraid. Staring across the table into his deep gray eyes, she knew she could. Not that it would be wise. Not that she would. She simply knew she might. That was troubling enough.

With trembling hands, she held on to her anger, her resistance. Touching her slightly rounded stomach, she refused to make another foolish mistake. As she had with James. As she had with Brody before her marriage. She'd done a lot of growing up since then, especially in the past few months. With careless bumps and bruises and more painful scars and scrapes to show for her foolishness, she'd learned her lessons the hard way.

Now the stakes had been raised. She wouldn't be

the only one hurt by reckless decisions made in the heat of the moment. *If* she ever decided to remarry, she'd have to be one hundred percent sure. No questions. No doubts. No mistakes.

But it was a moot point. She was *not* in love with Brody. And she was not going to fall in love with him, either.

Fitting the key into the lock, Brody unlocked the door to her room. Jillian stood next to him in the shrinking confines of the hallway. Sounds magnified. She heard the metal key slide into the brass knob, the chambers shift into place, the lock give. The hinges creaked. Her heart raced. Blood roared in her ears.

Say good-night and close the door. Quick.

Eager to end the evening, she stepped over the threshold. For some reason she felt like a teenager on her first date.

This is not a date.

A nervous giggle gurgled in her throat, making the moment more awkward. "Seems weird that we don't have any luggage."

"Uh-huh." His gaze was intense, his body too close.

Her nerves rattled against each other. "I guess we'll—I mean, I'll have to sleep in my clothes."

"Not necessarily," he said, his voice dipping low, offering a suggestion she didn't want to consider or him to imagine. Not that he would. But he was looking at her as if he could devour her in one blink.

Heat flashed inside her. "Well, um, thanks, Brody, for dinner. For, uh, everything. I—I haven't been out in a long while."

Shut up! He doesn't need to know that.

"You shouldn't be alone, Jillie. Maybe in the future you won't be." The sureness in his tone made her feel suddenly weak.

"Uh, um, I guess I'll see you in the morning."

"Or in the dunny." He gave her a flirtatious wink that sent her pulse skittering. "Ladies first, though."

He poked his head into her room, and she stepped back. Still only a foot separated them but she could feel his heat through her clothes, making her skin tingle.

"That must be the door to the dunny." He nodded toward a far door. "The manager said there's shampoo and soap. Even spare toothbrushes. Must have a lot of spur-of-the-moment travelers. Just give a knock when you're through."

"Sure. Okay." She put her hand on the door as if to close it. But he didn't back away. She felt the pulse at the base of her throat leap erratically as his gaze settled on her mouth.

He's going to kiss me.

Yes! A delightful shiver rippled down her spine.

No! Oh, heavens. No!

Her body went rigid with indecision. Her need, her desire, frightened her more than the possibilities of kissing Brody, of melting into his arms, of where a kiss might lead. Her gaze cut to the side, and she saw the wide bed waiting...waiting...waiting. She swallowed over the hard lump in her throat.

"Brody—" She stopped him from moving closer with a hand against his chest. Her hand itched to curl inward, to grab his shirt, to pull him toward her. She could feel the urgency of the hormones surging through her, making her imagine things, feel things, think things that she shouldn't be contemplating, experiencing or wishing for.

"Jillie." His Aussie tongue rolled over the contours of her name as his bare hand had once explored her body.

Stop this insanity, Jillian, right this minute! She didn't want another relationship. Especially with Brody. Kissing him, falling in love with him, made about as much sense as bungee jumping without a cord. She wouldn't fall for the same untrustworthy, pulsating desire again. She had to stop him.

But how?

He tilted his head, angled his mouth toward hers. Her lips tingled with need. Her heart pounded with hope. Her mind raced with fear.

Panicked, she blurted, "Brody, stop!" She flung the words at him as her last defense. "I'm pregnant."

A strange look entered his eyes, turning them dark as a winter sky. His features froze. His gaze cut downward to stare at her abdomen then back to her face.

Oh, God! What had she done now?

Eight

"You're what?" Brody asked, his voice faltering.

"Pregnant." Saying it out loud finally felt right. An inner strength awakened inside her. She could handle this. If she lost her job, she'd manage. Her confidence grew.

He peered down at her belly again, this time lingering, searching for a clue. When his gaze returned to her face, his eyes were burning.

"You picked a helluva time to tell me." The sharp anger in his voice made her flinch.

What had she expected? More importantly, what had she wanted from him? Her emotions shifted with uncertainty. "I know."

"Why didn't you tell me sooner?" His voice deepened with betrayal. "Why didn't you tell me?"

She shrugged, knowing the reason but afraid to voice it. Trembling, she said, "I was afraid. Afraid I'd lose my job."

Incredulous, he leaned forward, his breath punching her with emphasis. "You'll always have a job as long as you want one."

His words gave her a modicum of relief but fueled her temper with more fire. Her emotions seesawed, and she blamed it on the pregnancy hormones surging inside her. Not her uncertainty. Definitely not Brody.

"Because I'm pregnant?" she challenged. "Or because I'm a valued employee?"

He rubbed his jaw. His palm made a rasping sound as it stroked the dark stubble. "Jillie, you take the cake. You're scared to tell me you're pregnant because you think you'll lose your job. Then you're mad as a Tasmanian devil because you think your pregnancy might afford you special privileges. Which is it?"

"Both."

He gave a bold, uncompromising laugh, setting her nerves on edge. His eyes glittered like silver. The lines bracketing his mouth creased his taut cheeks when he afforded a brief smile, giving her an uneasy feeling in the pit of her stomach. "Figures. There's no way for me to answer that question, then, Jillie, without getting myself in trouble. But I'll give it my best shot."

His smile disappeared. "Because I know you."

His voice was husky, sexy... *No!* She shook loose his affect on her. He sounded serious, not sexy.

"Because I like to think of us as friends. Old friends. I want to believe you'll come to me in the future if you need help." He placed his hands on either side of the door frame. "Because I care for you, Jillie, probably more than either of us wants. I will do anything for you. All you have to do is ask."

Her body tightened, unsure how to respond. If only she could believe him. Her thoughts twisted with doubts. Would his caring, his concern, change anything? Unnerved by the aching in her heart, she felt hot tears scald the backs of her eyes while her spine stiffened with defiance. He cared? Did he even know how?

"But," he added, his voice cracking like a whip with strength and authority, "I wouldn't give you a job. I'd give you money if you asked, friendship, whatever you needed. But not a job. Not unless I knew you could do the work.

"And you can, Jillie." His gaze bore into her. "You're good. Impressive. You're in your element. If you couldn't do the job, I wouldn't hire you, even if you were my own mother. So don't ever let anyone tell you different. Not even your own doubts."

She swallowed the sharp knot in her throat. The truth of his words resonated through her, going deep, shaking apart her distrust. "Thank you, Brody. I appreciate that."

Taking a step forward, he stopped her from closing the door between them. His hand lifted as if to touch her, curling her insides with anticipation—no, dread—then he dropped his hand back to his side. Disappointment arced through her.

"Are you...doing okay?" he asked.

For the first time since she'd known him, he shifted from side to side as if uncomfortable inside his own skin, as if he, the handsome, sexy, well-known Brody Fortune, didn't know what to say, how to act. "I mean, is the pregnancy going well?"

His concern touched a tender need inside her. She nodded.

"Is that why you fainted? Not because of low blood sugar?"

"Yes." She sounded breathless.

"Have you been feeling ill much?"

Disconcerted with his intense inspection, she shrugged. ''A little. But I'm through my first trimester, so I'm feeling better. You don't have to worry about work.''

''I'm not. I'm worried about you…and the baby. You should have told me.'' His voice lightly scolded her. ''Will you tell me when…if you have trouble? If you feel sick? If you need anything?''

''Brody—''

''I mean it, Jillie.'' This time he touched her, cupped the side of her face, lifted her gaze to meet his when she would have looked away. ''I want to know. I want to help. Please…''

''All right,'' she said reluctantly, irritated by his insistence, frightened by her own need to lean on someone…on him.

''Good.'' He leaned closer, his breath brushing her face in a long, slow stroke.

Aware of all the years, all the questions, all the pain standing between them, she stared up at him, a need welling inside of her. He was going to kiss her. And God help her, she wanted it, welcomed it, even. Maybe it could be different between them now. Maybe…

He pressed his mouth to her forehead, tenderly, gently, brotherly. ''Get some sleep, love.''

Her heart throbbed with a new sorrowful ache as she watched him turn away and disappear into the room next door.

He'd kissed her like a brother. Not a lover.

With shock, she realized she much preferred thinking about Brody in an intimate way. Not as a boss.

Certainly not as a sibling. But any possibility of intimacy seemed as remote as the Australian Outback.

And it was her fault.

Brody paced his room, the length of his bed, his thoughts tossing and turning.

Jillie's pregnant. With James's baby!

He came to a halt beside the window and stared out at the night sky. Wispy gossamer curtains stretched across the blackness, shrouding the stars and moon. His soul felt dark, stormy, unpredictable.

Shucking his shirt, he tossed it onto a chair in the corner. One truth pounded inside his head…and heart. He cared for Jillian. More than he'd realized. More than he should.

After all those years of wondering if he'd made more out of her memory, if he'd conjured up feelings out of thin air, he knew his heart. But it brought him little comfort at the moment.

He'd told her the truth. He would do anything for her. Anything at all. Except…

A light rap on the door made his muscles tense. He realized it was her signal that she'd finished in the dunny. Needing a distraction from the direction of his thoughts, he jerked open the door.

A gasp resounded off the peach tiles. Jillian twisted around. Her startled eyes opened wide. She stood by the sink, clutching a towel to her chest. She looked rumpled, sexy.

No, he corrected, sweet. Maternal, right?

Having washed off what little makeup she wore, her face was bare. She curled her bare toes toward the tile floor. His gaze raked over her, noticing the stiffness in her neck, the tension in her hands, her white bra straps stark against her fair skin. His gaze shot back to her eyes, read the panic there.

Feeling a tightness, need, desire in his abdomen, he aimed his confusion at her. "You knocked."

"I did?" She shook her head. "N-no, no I didn't."

"I heard it."

Her gaze shifted toward her belt lying on the floor beside the door to his room. Understanding brightened her eyes. "My belt... I-it must have fallen off the doorknob. I didn't knock."

"I'm sorry, then." He started to back into his room, pulling the door closed between them. "I'll wait—"

"It's okay. I'm leaving." She reached for her makeup bag on the counter.

The towel covering her chest started to slide. He caught sight of a well-rounded breast pushed above the lacy top of her bra. His heart started to jackhammer. Feeling like a gawking teenager, he discreetly averted his gaze.

She clutched the towel to her.

"Um...uh," he stammered, "maybe I better wait outside."

She gave a terse nod, her eyes wide. "I'll gather up my things. Th-then it's all yours."

He started to turn away.

Again she stopped him with, "Brody, what's the procedure—er, plan for tonight. I mean, how will we know if one of us needs to...to use...to come into the..."

"Knocking first is always a good idea. I'll do that next time."

A heated blush rose on her cheeks. "Good."

Questions piqued his curiosity, his concern about her condition. He'd never been around a pregnant woman. He wondered when her stomach would swell. How long would it be until she'd be a mother? She certainly didn't look very far along. "Do you get up often in the night?"

"More than I used to," she answered. "But I guess it'll only get worse from here on out."

Not knowing anything about pregnancy, he simply nodded and stepped back into his room. He waited this time a full five minutes after he heard a distinct knock. When silence met his inquiring knock, he entered the dunny again.

He tried not to think about her on the other side of the door, sliding between the sheets. Had she removed the rest of her clothes? Or covered herself after the towel incident?

It didn't matter. He couldn't—wouldn't—think of her in that way. She was pregnant, for God's sake! She wasn't sexy. She was pregnant. With another man's baby.

But he couldn't get the image of her wrapped in that damn thick towel out of his head. Later, as he lay on top of his sheets, the ceiling fan sifting cold air over his naked body, he burned with an intensity he could only blame on Jillian. He'd never felt so much for any woman. He knew he'd loved her once. And he believed he could love her again.

But one thing stood between them. The baby. James's baby.

Guilt wrapped around him, strangled him. He cursed himself, forced himself to look deeply for the answers to the question that plagued him. Could he raise another man's child? James's child?

On the surface his fears seemed selfish, priggish, ludicrous. But they were all too real for him to ignore. He knew the pain and damage his own father had suffered. Teddy had been raised by his uncaring, overbearing grandfather. There was no question that Brody could ever treat a child that way himself.

But then, he also knew his brother Griff. The Fortunes had adopted him after they'd found him as a young child wandering on their property like a lost puppy. In spite of the unconditional love Brody's family had offered Griff, he'd never truly joined the family. He'd kept himself distant. That's what worried Brody now.

Would Jillian's child always feel awkward and distant toward a stand-in father?

Maybe his fears were irrational. Or maybe fate had stepped in once again. Maybe it was good he'd learned of her pregnancy before he'd kissed her again, before he'd taken their relationship to a new level, before he'd made another mistake.

But could he follow his first instinct and walk away now? A hollowness opened inside his chest, and more questions and doubts filled the empty spaces.

Where the hell was she?

Clint Lockhart waited at the designated spot. With the tips of his fingers, he flicked another cigarette butt onto the rocky ground beside Betsy's battered Ford. A dozen or so cigarette butts lay among the ashes and dirt like a jumble of headstones in a cemetery. The end of the latest cigarette sparked red, hot, angry. He crushed it with the toe of his boot.

Damn. He glanced at his watch. She said she'd be here at three. It was already three-thirty. His insides twitched.

Had she lied? Had she turned him in? He gave a look over his shoulder, searching for any cars or helicopters. As far as he could see, he was alone. This stretch of deserted land was rugged, rocky, treacherous, dotted only by sparse cedar.

Hell, Betsy wasn't going to turn him in. She loved him. At least, that's what she'd said. Not that you could ever put a woman's words in your wallet and bank on them. Still she hated the cops as much as he did.

But you could never trust anybody.

He struck another match on his belt buckle and lit the end of the cigarette, sucking in the bitter taste. He'd made sure Betsy believed her romantic feelings toward him were mutual. He'd hinted they had a future together. Readjusting his cowboy hat, angling the brim to shade his face from the glare of the sun, he chuckled to himself at how gullible some women... most women...could be. Hell, that was something he could count on, like finding spare change in sofa cushions.

He heard the sputtering of the engine first. Toward the end of the two-mile stretch of road he'd been watching, he saw a puff of hazy smoke. Slowly, a faded red truck came into view, rattling toward him.

Yanking open the driver's door, he slid behind the steering wheel of Betsy's car, careful not to bump his sore leg. He started the engine and waited. His hand hovered near the gearshift, his foot poised above the gas pedal. Just in case.

He watched in the rearview mirror as the truck approached. It stopped about fifty yards away. The hood shook as the truck idled.

After a couple of minutes, with Clint's nerves stretched taut as barbed wire, Betsy climbed out of the cab, gave a wave toward the driver of the truck who'd given her a lift and a recommendation at the Double Crown, then started toward him. He kept his gaze on the truck as it turned and headed back down the road it had come, puffs of smoke coughing out the exhaust pipe. When he was sure the driver was gone, he alighted from the car.

"Well?" he asked.

She gave him one of her lopsided grins. Red lipstick smeared her front tooth. The sun shone on her dusty brown locks. "I got it. I start work at the Fortune ranch tomorrow, cleaning in the big house."

He gave a whoop of delight. Hauling her into his arms, he twirled her around, feeling her bony frame rub against him suggestively. He preferred a woman with more meat on her bones, with more curves, with big boobs. But hell, he couldn't complain too much. At least she was willing. And eager.

"You were right," she said, breathless. "They needed lots of extra help what with that wedding coming up."

With a kiss square on her smiling mouth, he felt her melt against him like sugar in the rain. "Come on," he said, feeling as if the dark clouds over his head were suddenly breaking apart, "Let's go celebrate."

He could almost taste his sweet revenge on the Fortunes.

GET 2

HOW TO GET YOUR
2 FREE BOOKS AND FREE GIFT!

1. Peel off the MIRA® sticker on the front cover. Place it in the space provided at right. This automatically entitles you to receive two free books and an exciting surprise gift.

2. Send back this card and you'll get 2 "The Best of the Best™" books. These books have a combined cover price of $11.98 or more in the U.S. and $13.98 or more in Canada, but they are yours to keep absolutely FREE!

3. There's no catch. You're under no obligation to buy anything. We charge nothing – ZERO – for your first shipment. And you don't have to make any minimum number of purchases – not even one!

4. We call this line "The Best of the Best" because each month you'll receive the best books by some of today's most popular authors. These authors show up time and time again on all the major bestseller lists and their books sell out as soon as they hit the stores. You'll like the convenience of getting them delivered to your home at our special discount prices . . . and you'll love your *Heart to Heart* subscriber newsletter featuring author news, horoscopes, recipes, book reviews and much more!

5. We hope that after receiving your free books you'll want to remain a subscriber. But the choice is yours – to continue or cancel, anytime at all! So why not take us up on our invitation, with no risk of any kind. You'll be glad you did!

6. And remember…we'll send you a surprise gift ABSOLUTELY FREE just for giving THE BEST OF THE BEST a try.

SPECIAL FREE GIFT!
We'll send you a fabulous surprise gift, absolutely FREE, simply for accepting our no-risk offer!

Visit us online at
www.mirabooks.com

® and TM are registered trademarks of Harlequin Enterprises Limited.

BOOKS FREE!

THE BEST OF THE BEST™ — Here's How it Works:

If offer card is missing write to: The Best of the Best, 3010 Walden Ave., P.O. Box 1867, Buffalo, NY 14240-1867

BUSINESS REPLY MAIL
FIRST-CLASS MAIL   PERMIT NO. 717-003   BUFFALO, NY

POSTAGE WILL BE PAID BY ADDRESSEE

THE BEST OF THE BEST
3010 WALDEN AVE
PO BOX 1867
BUFFALO NY 14240-9952

NO POSTAGE
NECESSARY
IF MAILED
IN THE
UNITED STATES

* * *

"Have a seat," Brody instructed as Jillian brought him the files he needed. They'd been back at the office for a week now, but their routine seemed less and less predictable. The merger was coming together. It was his emotions that were falling apart. "Let's go over these figures."

But his mind wasn't on the merger. It was on Jillian. Only because he worried about her condition, he assured himself.

Over the past week he'd started to notice pale blue circles under her eyes. She'd begun wearing either full skirts or loose tops that hid the tiny bulge in her abdomen. Often he found himself staring at her figure, wondering about the changes, wishing he could put his hand on her stomach and feel the tiny life beginning inside her.

Mostly, he wondered and worried about whether she ate enough, slept enough. Who would take care of her? Was he working her too much? He knew if he suggested she take a little time off, she'd accuse him of coddling her. And she wouldn't accept it.

Convincing himself he was only worried about her welfare, he said, "Jillie, have dinner with me tonight."

Her startled gaze met his across the top of his desk. The blue in her eyes softened then sparked with indignation. "I thought we were going to go over these numbers."

"We are. We could finish over dinner."

"I don't think so." She dragged her gaze back to the papers in her lap.

"To which question? Going over the numbers, or dinner?"

Annoyance made her chin jut out. "It wasn't a question. It was a command."

"It's *your* decision."

"Good. Then, no. Thank you, though."

He frowned. "That's not the answer I wanted."

"I know." She opened the folder on her lap and studied the printout of the Australian holdings.

Her softening shape, the determination in the angle of her chin, the way her soft, blond hair cupped the edge of her jaw made him want to wrap her in his arms and kiss her until they were both senseless. Trying to ignore her and the need inside him, he shuffled the papers on his desk. "It's not what you think."

"What?" Her brow creased.

"My asking you to dinner."

"And what am I thinking?" she challenged.

"It's not a date."

Relief—or maybe disappointment—flickered in the depths of her eyes. She waited for him to finish.

"Uh, not at all." His mind raced. What the hell was it, then? "I need your help."

"To cut your steak?" Humor laced her words.

He grinned at her, liking her tart sense of humor. "It's Matilda."

She arched an eyebrow at him. "Your sister?"

"I don't know what to do with her." The real worries about his sister intruded momentarily on his concerns—and desires—for Jillian. He raked his fingers through his hair and leaned back in his leather chair.

"I invited her to stay the weekend with me here in San Antonio. I feel like I'm trying to baby-sit a twenty-one-year-old."

"You are."

"I know. I know. But it's for her own good." He felt a weight descend on his shoulders. "I'm worried about her. She's a little dynamo. Wouldn't surprise me if she got tangled up with the first American who came along. Probably some cowboy."

"And that would be bad?"

"At her age, she shouldn't be making that kind of decision."

"At your age," she countered, "you should know you can't do anything to stop her. It's not your decision, Brody. It's hers."

His eyebrows compressed into a frown. Just as marrying James had been Jillian's decision. Irritation snapped his jaw shut. This conversation was not going the way he wanted. Jillian was not cooperating. Not that she ever had. She'd always been a challenge. Maybe that's one reason he'd always been intrigued by her.

"Are we going to go over these figures?" she asked, impatience entering her voice.

"Sure." He stood and came around his desk, hiking his hip onto the edge of the solid wood. He inhaled the scent of her light, breezy fragrance and felt a pulsing need deep inside him. "Maybe you could help me. With her...Matilda."

Jillian stared up at him, her lips parted, making him remember his mouth slanted against hers. "How do you mean?"

He cleared his throat, tried to erase the image from

his mind. "Well, you seem to understand the situation."

"Brody—"

"You could be an intermediary. A friend to her. A voice of reason for me. She's all alone in town."

"I thought she was staying at the ranch."

"She was. But after many phone calls last week, I convinced her to come visit. I wanted to give Griff a break."

"You've been talking to her on the phone?" Her question was almost as ludicrous as the tremor in her voice.

"Yeah."

"Is she the woman who's been calling you?"

He gave her a questioning look. "What woman?"

"The one with an Aussie accent."

He thought for a moment then grinned. "Yeah."

Jillie gave an awkward laugh. "Oh, well, I wish she had said hello."

Confused by her questions but also cheered by them, he asked, "Does that mean you'll help me?"

"You're just giving Griff a break from spying on her."

"We're not spying."

"Guarding, then," she said in a disbelieving tone. "What do you need me for? She has you to act as a watchdog."

He shrugged off her comment. "Right. She'd like to ditch her big brother. She doesn't have any girlfriends here in the States. There's no one at the ranch even close to her age. Except cowboys. You could be like a big sister to her. I bet she'd enjoy talking to you, seeing you again."

"No pressure, right?" Her mouth quirked in the semblance of a smile.

"You said yourself you hadn't been out much. You're new in town, too. You know how lonely that can be." He played his last trump card, hoping more than anything that she would finally agree to help him, knowing it really had nothing to do with his little sister. "You'd be a big help."

She tapped her pen against the folder, irritation making the cadence brisk. "Is this a job requirement?"

"No. It's strictly your decision."

She sighed heavily. "What would I have to do?"

"Have dinner with us tomorrow night. Nothing fancy. No strings attached."

A long silence stretched between them, unraveling his nerves. If she declined, he didn't know what he'd do. He had to see her outside of work. He had to know more about her, how she was coping. He had to make sure she was okay.

He needed to be with her. Not as boss and employee. Not as friends. And it scared the hell out of him.

"Okay," she said with resignation. "I guess it couldn't hurt anything. But only this once."

Nine

"**I**'m definitely man crazy!"

Brody glared at Matilda and gritted his teeth.

Men! Couldn't his sister think of anything else?

Holding a tray of two-inch-thick Porterhouse steaks, he backed through the opening onto the patio of his high-rise apartment. The view of San Antonio with the amber reflection of the setting sun blazing off the surrounding buildings was romantic, making him wish he and Jillie were alone.

But would that be right? How could he pursue anything with the baby on the way? Did he even want to?

Suddenly angry—with himself, with fate—he slammed the screen door closed but kept his hearing pinned to the women's conversation. They sat around the wrought-iron patio table beneath a spinning ceiling fan. Sweat beaded along his spine as the heat pressed in on him. Needing a drink, he set down the tray, grabbed up his beer, tipped back his head and took a deep, long pull.

"So—" Matilda crossed her jeans-clad legs and leaned forward "—where do you go, Jillian, in San Antonio to meet men?"

Brody choked, coughed and banged the beer bottle on the side ledge of his barbecue grill. Men were off-limits to his sister, or so he wished. That was the easiest way to protect her. And the thought of Jillian pursuing some man, *any* man other than him, turned his stomach inside out.

He'd hoped getting his sister and Jillian together would have been good for all concerned. Now he wasn't so sure.

"Are you all right?" Jillian called to him as he sputtered and coughed again.

He gave a grim nod, forked a steak and set it on the grill. The meat sizzled and popped like his nerves.

"I don't get out much." Jillian leaned back into the cushioned chair and continued her conversation with Matilda. "I haven't lived in San Antonio long enough to know where to look for men." She gave Brody a sidelong glance and seemed too pleased with the topic of conversation.

Brody felt a jarring sense of panic. Did she want to go looking for men? Or was she nettling him with his sister's manhunt?

For two women who seemed so different, he thought, they sure had found a common ground. Jillian was the epitome of femininity in her soft flowing skirts and carefully styled blond hair. While his sister was a tomboy, in her jeans, boots, and wildly waving blond tresses. For two opposites and relative strangers, who had only met once ten years ago, they acted as if they were long lost friends. He clenched his jaw. Wasn't that what he'd wanted?

"Maybe we should go out together." Matilda sipped the frozen Margarita she'd made in Brody's blender. "Really kick up our heels. See the sights. Meet some men."

Sirens went off in Brody's brain, sending galvanizing sparks along his spine. He froze, his hand gripping the steak fork hard as he waited for Jillian's response.

Jillian slanted a mischievous gaze toward Brody as she sipped her sparkling water. "That might be fun."

Aggravated and distressed, Brody realized his sister had the moves—and the looks—that would attract men like koalas to a eucalyptus tree. The realization that she was a full-grown woman with a body to prove it set his teeth on edge.

And Jillian! Hell, if the two of them set out to find men, Brody had no doubts they'd attract a Texas truckload of willing cowboys.

He'd hoped Jillian would act as a good influence on Matilda, but now he was beginning to think the reverse was happening. What would he do if they wanted to go out shopping for men? Could he stop them? His shoulders bunched with anger. And he could only aim it at himself.

He had to protect his sister. But a stronger, more urgent need to protect Jillian shot through him, too. From herself, even. But how? And why? Hell, he wasn't sure about anything anymore.

Matilda stood up from the table, stretching her arms wide, arching her back. "It feels so good to be free from the ranch. The security out there is tighter, more restrictive, than a training bra."

"Matilda!" Brody called a warning.

"Well, it is!" She gave a huff of indignation. "Just because some loony-tune is on the loose…what's his name?"

"Clint Lockhart. And he's not a loon. He's an escaped convict. A murderer."

"Who is this?" Jillie asked, alarm arching her eyebrows.

Brody took a deep breath, closed the barbecue lid on the steaks and walked toward the women. He squared his shoulders. Maybe he could scare a little common sense into Jillie if not Matilda. "The man murdered Uncle Ryan's second wife, Sophia."

Jillie's mouth opened with shock.

"He had been arrested and was in prison. During a prisoner transfer the police car wrecked and he bailed," he continued, determined to drive home his point that the real world of strange men and crazy notions was not safe. "He's been out on the loose since. But the police think he's in the area."

Matilda rolled her eyes and yawned with disinterest. "Uncle Ryan's worried this guy might show up at the ranch."

Brody scowled at his little sister. "We should all be taking extra precautions. Lockhart hates the Fortunes. Believes they stole his birthright out from under him when they bought his family's ranch."

"See!" Matilda exclaimed. "It has nothing to do with me."

"It has everything to do with you. You're a Fortune. He could exact his revenge—if that's what he's looking for—on any one of us if he thought it would hurt Uncle Ryan."

"Oh, he's probably a million miles from here." Matilda turned away, exasperated. "You and Griff need to stop worrying so much."

"It's my job to worry, little sister. About the family. And especially about you. Get used to it.'' Now he had Jillie to worry about, too.

Matilda gave a huff of indignation and Brody stalked back to check the steaks.

Whispering as if he couldn't hear them, Matilda confided to Jillian, "He thinks he's so smart. Mr. Know-it-all." She plopped down on the cushioned chair. "If I would've known Brody was going to act like Griff I wouldn't have bothered to come to San Antonio to visit."

"He's just trying to protect you," Jillian said.

Brody nodded, silently agreeing with her, hoping she'd continue in that vein.

"He's just being bossy," Matilda complained. "I wish he'd get married—like Reed. Then he wouldn't worry about me so much. It's going to be dull as dirt around here."

"Not necessarily," Jillian said. "Maybe I can enlist your help while you're here."

Brody tensed, his hand paused in lifting the lid to the barbecue. Now what?

"To help find you a man?" Matilda laughed. "I always thought you and Brody would get married. What ever happened between you two?"

Jillian's shocked glance met his. His spine was as straight as a metal spike as he anticipated her answer.

He looked away, busied himself turning the steaks, and mumbled to himself, "It's none of your damn business."

"Oh, it's a long story," Jillian answered for him. Did he hear regret in her voice? She fiddled with her skirt, straightening the hem, pinching the seams between nervous fingers.

Suddenly he wanted to hear her version of their past. Something had come between them, something more than her mother's sudden illness. Otherwise why hadn't she told him? Why hadn't she cried on his shoulder? Why hadn't she turned to him when her mother died, instead of James? The questions burned like red-hot coals in his gut. *Because you were thousands of miles away.*

"Just wasn't meant to be," Jillian said in a distant, remote voice that made him wonder if fate had kept them apart for a reason. Or if it had all been a mistake.

"Really?" Matilda crossed her legs and leaned forward, propping her chin on her hands. "You both seemed so much in love. And Brody never would talk about what happened. I must have asked him a million times why you went back to the States, why he didn't go after you."

Despite the Texas heat, a cold sweat broke out on Brody's forehead. He remembered the shock, the sharp pain, the barbs of betrayal he'd felt when he'd gone to pick Jillian up that long-ago night. He'd made special plans for them—reservations at a sleek, upscale restaurant that offered candlelight and romantic music, then a suite at the finest hotel in Sydney. He'd wanted the night to be special, magical…when they finally made love. His heart still ached with distrust over her sudden desertion. If he allowed himself to fall in love with her once more, would she bail again?

Jillian's complexion flushed along her neck and cheeks. "It doesn't matter now anyway."

"No more sparks, then?" Matilda asked, getting too personal for Brody's peace of mind.

He gave a slight negative shake of his head, denying the attraction to Jillian, but he couldn't ignore the truth blazing inside him, turning him inside out each time he looked at her. Hell, there were enough sparks between Jillie and himself to start a fire that could consume all of Texas...even Australia.

"Or are you involved with someone else now?" Matilda's obsession with love and romance—especially his and Jillie's—grated on Brody's nerves.

He squinted at Jillian who sat as still as a Texas summer breeze. She looked pale, distraught. Damn, he should have told Matilda about Jillian's recent loss of her husband. But he'd thought the women would discuss clothes and makeup, maybe a recipe or two. Frowning at his sister, he should have known better.

"No," Jillian answered, her lips compressed. Then she shrugged and stared down at her lap. Her hair fell forward, veiling her delicate features. She looked lost and very much alone. His heart ached for her. "Well, I guess you could say I'm involved. Or will be."

"With whom?"

Her hands covered her lower abdomen. Lifting her head, she smiled softly...maternally. Brody felt a catch in his chest. "With my baby."

"Ohmygosh!" Matilda jumped up from her seat. "You're pregnant!"

Jillian nodded. "Almost four months now."

"Oh! That's wonderful!" Wrapping her arms across her middle, Matilda contained her enthusiasm. His little sister showed more compassion and understanding than Brody would have given her credit for when she placed a hand on Jillian's knee. "It is wonderful, isn't it?"

"Yes." Jillian's eyes and voice filled with tears and flooded Brody's soul with regrets that the baby wasn't his. "It is."

"Who's the father?"

"Matilda—" A cold knot settled in the pit of his stomach.

"Oh, I know it's none of my business. I just…I'm so excited for you."

"Thank you," Jillian said, a warm glow entering her eyes. "I'm a widow. My husband died this summer." At Matilda's gasp, Jillian covered his sister's hand with her own. "It's okay. I'm okay." A firm conviction rang in her voice.

"I'm so sorry, Jillian." Matilda's voice filled with tears. "And here I've been going on and on about men."

"Don't worry about it." Jillian gave her a soothing smile. "No worries," she added the easy Australian phrase.

"What can I do to help? Would you like a baby shower?" When Jillian shook her head, Matilda kept on. "How about help with the nursery? I've always wanted to decorate a nursery. We'll have so much fun buying sweet little clothes. A teddy bear. Every baby needs a teddy bear."

Jillian leaned back in her chair, blinked away the tears and laughed. The lovely sound of her laughter brought much-needed relief. "I'd love it if you helped me. I was going to invite you to do just that."

"Just imagine how your life is going to change. It's going to be so wonderful." His sister got a dreamy look in her gray eyes that alarmed Brody. "We'll help make it wonderful. Won't we, Brody?"

He gave an affirmative nod, his throat clogged with uncertain emotions.

"I've always wanted a baby," Matilda added.

Brody's hand faltered as he lifted a steak off the grill.

"Just find a good man first. I didn't. Even though my marriage was less than perfect, it's like I've been given a second chance with this baby." Maternal love filled Jillian's voice. "Don't make the same mistakes I did."

"Oh, Jillian," Matilda said, her voice softening, "I'm so sorry. I didn't mean—"

"It's okay. I know what you meant. And I appreciate it. I wish more than anything that I was married, that I wasn't bringing this baby into the world alone. I know what it's like to grow up without a father. But I guess we can't have everything we want."

Brody's nerves electrified. Was Jillian looking for a husband? Marriage? He had a sudden urge to make it happen for her—to become her husband—to offer her exactly what she wanted. But did she want him?

And is that what he wanted? An instant family?

Before he could make a fool of himself, reason and logic kicked into gear and he took an emotional step back. Doubts mingled with regret and fears. The baby she carried should have been his. Jillian should have been his wife. But she wasn't. She never had been. Never would be.

"Just don't rush into marriage," Jillian continued. "Like I did. Take your time. You're so young. Find the right man first."

Brody's heart contracted at Jillian's words. She had found the right man first, he thought. Him. But she'd left him and married James instead. Anger shot through him. He'd never forgive himself for letting his pride stop him from going after her. Now it was too damn late.

"Maybe I can help you find a good man," Matilda offered. "There are a lot of men at the ranch."

Jillian chuckled. "Oh, yeah, right. In a month or so I'll really be showing. I'm sure some man wants to be with a big, fat pregnant lady. How romantic." She shook her head. "No, thanks. Even though I wish I could fall in love with someone wonderful and he would love helping to raise my child, I've resigned myself to the facts. It's a lot of responsibility for someone to take on.

"This is my doing." Jillian's voice gained assurance and strength. "This baby is mine. I'll raise it alone."

Stabbing the steaks with the tines of the serving fork, Brody lifted them off the grill and onto a broad platter. Guilt suffocated him. She spoke with wisdom. It was a lot of responsibility for a man who was not the father. Maybe too much. Angry at himself for his selfish attitude, he slid the screen to the side too hard and it screeched.

Both women looked up, as if startled he was still around, as if they'd forgotten he was listening. Jillian's blue eyes were round and sparkling. He wanted to go to her, tell her everything would be okay, he'd take care of her, of her baby. But something inside him held him back. An emotion he didn't recognize and didn't admire trapped him. He couldn't promise what she wanted.

Matilda sighed. "I just don't believe any of that. I

think any man would be eager to marry you.'' She looked to Brody for help. ''Don't you?''

''Dinner's ready,'' he said, uneasy.

''You definitely need to come to Reed and Mallory's wedding next weekend.'' Matilda led Jillian into the apartment. ''Right, Brody?''

''Did you check the spuds?'' he asked, putting the platter of steaks on the dining table and heading toward the kitchen.

''Wouldn't you like to come to the wedding?'' Matilda asked, pushing.

''I, um, don't think it would be…polite,'' Jillian stammered, ''I mean, since I don't know the bride or groom.''

''Nonsense. It's not like you'll be crashing the wedding. We'll get you a date.''

''Oh, I don't think—'' Jillian tried to stop Matilda.

But his little sister didn't pay attention. ''Okay, an escort.'' She trailed after Brody. ''Hold on there, big brother.'' She grabbed his arm and turned him around.

Over his little sister's head, his gaze met Jillian's. Wide and uncertain, her eyes stayed on him, searching his face, probing his heart, seeking his help.

''Don't you think Jillian should go? It would be good for her.'' Matilda snapped her fingers with sudden inspiration. ''I have a brilliant idea. Jillian needs someone who won't monopolize her time. She needs to feel free to meet the single men at the wedding.'' She glanced over her shoulder at Jillian. ''Right?''

''I don't think…'' Jillian paused, hesitant and awkward.

''And of course, the best person for that job is

Brody. You can introduce her to men and then ske-daddle so you won't be a threat.''

His hand closed into a fist. He'd threaten whom-ever he wanted. Whenever he wanted. Especially if it had to do with Jillian.

"So you'll take her to the wedding? Won't you?" Matilda pushed.

What could he say? No? Yes? Oh, hell. He was caught. "I suppose. That is, if she wants to go, I'd want to be the one to take her."

Maybe she'd back out.

"Well?" Matilda looked to Jillian. "Is that all right with you?"

Jillian had the look of a kangaroo caught in the headlights. As if she couldn't escape, either. Shrug-ging, she said, "If you're sure I won't be intruding on the celebration."

Matilda clapped her hands. "Then it's settled. Jil-lian you now officially have a date…er, escort for the wedding." His sister shot him a steely-eyed glance. "And you, sport, better be on your best behavior. Treat her right. You hear?"

"My pleasure," he stated, sensing it might be his punishment.

"Brody, you—"
"Jillie—"

They spoke simultaneously, sitting side by side in his rented sports car. Jillian clasped her purse in her lap. If she shifted too much in the supple leather bucket seat her shoulder would brush his. She already knew how strong and vibrant he felt. She didn't need any reminders.

What had she agreed to? A date with Brody? To a wedding? Oh, heavens! How could she get out of it?

Hooking his wrist over the steering wheel, he tilted his head toward her. He gave her a crooked, engaging smile. "Go ahead. You first."

"No, it's okay. What were you going to say?" She blinked, feeling as nervous as a sixteen-year-old on her first date. Maybe he'd back out before she had to.

He shifted the car into gear and brushed back a lock of black hair that had fallen across his forehead. "I wanted to apologize for Matilda."

She almost breathed a sigh of relief. Here goes. Brody must be feeling just as trapped as she was. Now he was going to back out and make it easy on her. But for some crazy reason, disappointment choked her.

That's what you want, isn't it? You want him to back out—back off—move out of your life and make your life simple again.

She wasn't sure anymore. *No, of course, that's how I want it.* She didn't want to date Brody. Even a pretend date. Especially a pretend date. Or was it the "pretend" part that she objected to the most? *Heaven, help me!*

"Matilda gets charged about certain topics," Brody continued, accelerating as they sped up the ramp onto the highway leading to her home. "Specifically men. She's always been boy crazy, now she's *man* crazy and that's much worse."

Jillian stared at him, confused by his choice of words, intrigued by the sure, confident way he turned the wheel and the boldness with which he shifted gears.

"I should have told her about James…or warned you…" He shoved his fingers through his hair, leaving tufts standing on end. She had an urge to smooth his hair back into place but resisted. "Hell, I shouldn't have let her go on like that about finding a man for you."

"It's all right," Jillian said, wondering how long it was going to take for him to get around to backing out of their date.

"No, it's not." His voice deepened with what sounded like regret and a good measure of angst. His hands tightened on the steering wheel, making the veins on the back of his hand prominent. "And it's my fault."

"Really—" she placed her hand on his arm, briefly, but long enough to feel the tension in him and a spark of electricity sizzle through her "—it's okay." She pulled her hand away.

"Matilda's got this notion that she wants to get married and have a family right away. But it seems like every man she goes out with is…lacking."

Jillian imagined what it would be like to have so many overprotective brothers. The image gave her a warm, cozy feeling inside. How she wished at times there was someone to care enough, to love her enough, to watch over her, to be concerned for her welfare. Someone sure and strong, bold and brave.

Her gaze slanted toward Brody. A deep longing welled up inside her. What would it be like for Brody to care that much for her? But not as a brother. As a lover. She wanted to feel his arms around her, his hands on her, to taste his kiss again. For him to be the one who'd help give her a family, a home.

Shaken by her need, she cut her eyes back to the road and watched the headlights slash through the darkness and the angry red brake lights flash in front of them. She slammed on the brakes of her speeding thoughts. She focused instead on Matilda, doubting his little sister enjoyed his protection.

Managing a forced laugh, she said, "Is that big brother talking? Somehow I doubt you Fortune brothers will approve of any man Matilda brings home."

He bristled. "If the man was decent we'd approve."

Jillian shook her head. "I don't think so."

"We're just trying to protect her from herself," Brody said. "She picks men who are too wild, who aren't interested in settling down. Men like...like your James."

As if jabbed with a red-hot poker, Jillian's defenses went on alert. "What do you mean by that?"

"You said it yourself. He fooled around on you. Drank too much. From what you told me back in college, I never thought he was worth much, anyway. The way he was always telling you how to dress, what to say, where to go, who to talk to."

"You're one to talk." She crossed her arms over her chest, fuming. *How dare he act like Mr. Perfect. When he was anything but!* "How dare you!"

"What?" He looked at her, then back at the road. "What did I say?"

"You of all people shouldn't be condemning James for his...cheating. Not when you've done it yourself."

His head snapped in her direction. He glared at her,

then forced himself to watch the road. "What the hell are you talking about?"

She couldn't help herself. Anger pumped through her veins until her body trembled with the effort to suppress her rage. She'd gone this far. She might as well confront him as she'd wanted to do years ago. "Did you forget about Gail?"

"Gail? Gail who?" He shook his head.

"Easy come, easy go, eh?" she said, not believing for a minute that he didn't know who she was speaking of. "Gail Harken. You remember her, don't you?"

"Gail Harken?" He stared at her, acting confused, when she knew he'd finally been caught.

"Yes. Tall, redhead, went to Winslow."

"Gail Harken?"

"Would you stop saying her name!" Her temperature reached the boiling level.

"What does she have to do with this?" he asked.

Anger burned inside her like a well-fueled furnace. Once more, the fury, hurt and humiliation ignited until she felt herself incinerating from the inside out. Maybe it was time she told him off for what he'd done. Maybe it would finally help her put Brody in her past where he belonged so she could go on with her life.

Gritting her teeth, she spelled it out for him. "You were sleeping with her when you were supposed to only be dating me."

Ten

Stunned by Jillian's accusation, Brody swerved the car to the shoulder of the road. The BMW came to a shrieking halt. Shock yielded to fury, and it hammered inside him to get out. He glared at her. "What the hell are you saying?"

Her eyes narrowed and her lips thinned with anger. "That you are just as bad as James. Maybe worse." Her voice caught. "I expected more from you. I believed you. I—I..."

He shook his head, confused by her words. "I don't understand. I wasn't dating Gail. We'd broken up before I started going out with you. Where did you get this crazy idea?"

She sucked in a shaky breath. "From the direct source—Gail. She came to see me the night...*that* night." She jerked her chin and stared out the passenger window. "Why am I bothering?"

He remembered *that* night as if it were yesterday. The night air had been scented with eucalyptus. The stars had glittered brightly. His pulse had hummed with anticipation of them going away together, of making love to Jillie for the first time. Because he'd known she was the woman he'd marry. When he'd gone to pick her up, his nervous excitement had become riddled with anxiety. He'd learned she'd bailed…gone back to the States. He still felt the impact—the roiling confusion, the crushing blow—as if it had happened yesterday.

His pulse echoed in his ears as he remembered Gail coming to him later, trying to comfort him. He'd pushed her away. Nobody, no woman could heal the crack in his heart. Except Jillian.

Now, she shoved a spike into that crack, widening it. How could she so easily have believed that lie?

She looked at him again, her eyes gleaming with defiance. "She told me you'd been two-timing both of us."

He cursed. He aimed the harsh words at Gail, at fate, at Jillian. "And you believed her?"

"N-not at first." Her eyes were round and full of unshed tears that made the blue shimmer. "I trusted you. And you know how hard it was for me to trust anybody…any man…after my daddy left." Her shoulders squared. "But I learned to trust you. I trusted you."

She blinked and twin teardrops spilled from her eyes and ran down her cheeks, marking a trail for the past and one for the future, erasing all that had been between them and the possibility of anything again.

Wild, chaotic emotions churned inside him, stirring up anger, bitterness, and deep penetrating sorrow. Why had she believed Gail? Why did fate have to play this ugly trick? How could he ever convince Jillian of the truth?

His anger narrowed on her. She'd believed a lie against him. A gross, outrageous lie that had no resemblance to the facts. Why had she so easily accepted Gail's word over his? He almost laughed but he couldn't get a sound through his closed windpipe. She hadn't even asked for his side of it! And she'd ruined their future together, by not trusting him. "Why didn't you come to me? Why didn't you ask me for the truth?"

Silence pounded inside the car as the questions lingered. No answer could bridge the gaping space that had separated them.

Without turning toward him, she said, "Because I knew you'd deny it. Just as you are now." Her voice shook as if she were reliving the rage. "I was angry, hurt, humiliated, and in no mood for empty denials."

He clenched his hands, tightening them around the steering wheel, as if he could choke the truth out of it. So much time had been wasted. So much had been lost. All because of a lie.

"You didn't even give me the benefit of the doubt. Not even enough to question me...to give us a chance."

"Would it have made a difference?"

"Maybe. It could have made all the difference in the world. If you would've given me a chance, instead of believing a damn lie."

She jerked her chin, moving further away from him. "I am not the guilty party here. Don't make me out to be the villain."

Immediately he knew a flat denial would be like a ball bouncing off a brick wall. She had closed her heart to him, to the truth, long ago. She had wanted to believe the lies. For whatever reason, she'd wanted to believe the worst about him. And she had. There was no convincing her now. A hollow ache throbbed in his chest.

"Gail told me what you'd been doing that weekend you said you had to go home to see your family. She told me how you both had gone off together…the way we were supposed to go away that night."

He shook his head, knowing he couldn't say anything to convince her otherwise. "So that's why you left school? Because you didn't want to face me." And that's why she'd married James.

"No." She sounded sharp. "I wanted to slap your face, to tell you off, to…" Shadows shrouded her face. As a car passed, its headlights gave him a glimpse at the stark pain in her eyes.

"I called home to talk to Mom, to tell her about…to cry on her shoulder." She gave an uncomfortable shrug. "That's when I learned she'd been taken to the hospital. She'd had a stroke."

Her belief in his betrayal combined with the loss of her mother must have been a devastating blow. His chest tightened as he imagined all she'd suffered.

Resignation clamped around his throat. "Then that's why you didn't bother to say goodbye."

She gave a slight nod. "I had to go home. To be with her."

He ran his palms over the supple leather encasing the steering wheel. Grief seized his throat, squeezing, strangling the last of his anger.

Regret defied logic, tunneled through his self-serving emotions to make room for one last question. What if he could convince Jillian that Gail had lied?

Could he undo the pain of the past? Or did it matter anymore? Yes, dammit, it did. He couldn't let her believe a lie. He couldn't let her believe he'd acted like James, that he'd cheated on her, that what they'd shared—their love—had been false. It had meant everything to him. She had changed his life. And her leaving had devastated him.

He shifted in his seat and faced her once more. The defiance gleaming in her eyes stabbed him. His temper bled red fury. He grabbed her by the arms, pulled her close until she couldn't hide, couldn't look away. He searched for some recognition of the truth.

"It was a lie, Jillie. A damn lie. I know you don't believe me. I have no proof but my word. Which probably means nothing to you. Not now. Not after James trampled on your vows. Not after your father deserted you." His heart bruised his breastbone, pounding, hammering, beating with determination. "But I swear to you that I was faithful to you. I loved you. More than I'd ever loved anybody. I never would have hurt you like that. I would have done anything for you." His voice faded, his strength drained out of him as he read disbelief in her eyes. "I still would."

He released her as suddenly as he'd grabbed her. "Hell, I can't convince you." He slumped back in his seat, defeated by the actions of others that resonated louder and stronger than his love ever could. "Damn! Damn Gail. Damn you for believing her."

The silent echo after Brody's censuring shook Jillian to her very foundation. She felt the walls around her heart shift and crack. What if Gail had lied? Suddenly events that had seemed so clear were now fuzzy and blurred. Had she even questioned whether Gail was telling the truth? Or had she jumped off a huge cliff into the wrong conclusion?

He shoved the gearshift into place, punched the accelerator and whipped the car back onto the highway.

The rumble of the engine couldn't drown out the roaring in her ears and pounding in her temples. She stared straight ahead, watching the headlights slice through the darkness the way his condemnation had slashed through her pain.

He didn't speak another word the rest of the drive. Her mind spun with questions. Her accusations turned inward. Doubts surfaced. She tried to assimilate all he'd told her, all he hadn't said, with his simple denial, with his blunt anger.

Was it her fault for believing Gail? Why had she so readily turned against Brody? Had a part of her wanted to condemn him as she'd condemned her own father for running out on her?

Then the truth ignited inside her. She'd wanted to run out on Brody. Before *he* could leave *her*. As she'd believed he eventually would.

She'd never understood why Brody Fortune, the most popular and best-looking man on campus, had wanted to be with her. Maybe that lack of self-esteem had undermined their relationship and condemned it from the beginning. Maybe it had just been a matter of time. If it hadn't been Gail, then it would have been something or someone else. She swallowed back bitter tears, choked down the what-ifs and maybes that welled up inside her.

Then another question blazed inside her. Had she married James because he would give her fears credence? She'd admitted to marrying him more for comfort and security than for love. He hadn't come through on anything she'd hoped or expected from him. Except that he'd cheated on her. In that, he'd proven her theory that love fails.

A deep sorrow welled up inside her. She must have sensed that Brody could hurt her more than anyone else ever had or ever could. And she'd taken the first opportunity to believe the worst, to make her escape. Before he could destroy her.

When Brody stopped the car in front of Amy's house, she remained unmoving in the passenger seat, unsure what to do or say. Jolted to the very core of her being, she couldn't find the strength to move or speak. The engine idled and she felt the vibrations throughout her body. She didn't know who to believe—Gail, Brody, even herself. Her own instincts were colored, tainted.

But she recognized one distinct possibility. A possibility that shattered the past and paved a way toward the future, illuminating it with uncertainty. She had jumped to conclusions. She'd taken the easiest path. And she'd been wrong.

She hadn't possessed the belief or trust in herself that someone could love her, stay with her, be true to her. And she'd paid a dear price.

"Brody, I..." She faltered, as she now did in her once firm convictions. Each uncertain word brought sharp pain. She couldn't go back. She was scared to go forward. But she couldn't stay where she was, alone in the dark and afraid. "I don't know what happened between you and Gail and—"

"I can tell you what happened. Nothing."

She tensed. His anger frayed her nerves. Her brow furrowed, and she gripped the door handle for strength, for support or for a way of escape. What had she done? What was she doing? Was she too afraid to face the truth? Too shaken to confront the possibility that she'd made another mistake? "But, I—"

"Believe what you want, Jillian. I can't convince you otherwise."

"I just want to understand what happened."

"I told you." He ground the words out between his teeth and leaned toward her until they were but a breath apart. "Nothing happened between Gail and me. There was nothing between us. Nothing. Ever.

"Yes, I dated her. For a short time. Before I knew you. Before you and I began seeing each other. But no, I didn't love her. I didn't care for her. Not the way I cared for you. Not the way I loved you.

"And no, I didn't go away with her for the weekend. I didn't make love to her. It was a lie. A fabricated lie she wove to get back at me. Or to get me back. I don't know which. I don't even care now.

"It worked, though." He gave a coarse laugh. "It convinced you. It destroyed me. And she won."

"Brody—"

"I didn't go back to Gail. I couldn't—" His voice broke off, hoarse and shattered. "Not after I'd gotten a taste of real..." He stopped himself. "Hell, I guess it was all a figment of my imagination. It doesn't matter anymore."

His voice injected venom into her heart. She felt the fear inside her shrivel and die. It did matter. His pain mattered to her, more than she would have believed.

Determination took root inside her heart. Looking into his iron-colored eyes, fortified with a strength and resilience she could barely comprehend, she recognized a new courage surfacing, growing inside her.

Not born of fear, but of hope. An urgent need claimed her, pounded inside her until her skin tingled and burned with intensity.

Pale light from a streetlamp softened the hard edges and sharp contours of his face. She wanted to touch him, to smooth away the creases in his brow, to erase the lines bracketing his mouth, pulling it tight. Her focus centered on him, his very essence, the man she'd known, the man she wanted to know again, and she remembered his gentleness, his intensity.

"Jillie," he said, his voice hoarse and rough, "go inside."

She shook her head, unable to move away from him, no longer able to retreat. She touched him then. He jerked but didn't move away. Her fingertips glided over the plane of his jaw, moving toward the corner of his mouth. The roughness of his skin awakened a need deep inside her. His clean scent stirred her desire. Tilting her head, she pressed her mouth against his.

At first he felt stiff, surprised, unsure. *Oh, what have I done now?*

She hesitated. Her insecurities tangled around her, entrapping her once more. She could hear his sharp, unsteady breaths. Her heart faltered.

Against her mouth he said, "Kiss me, Jillie. Like you mean it."

It was a challenge. She almost backed down, retreated. But not again. Not this time.

Acutely aware that she'd wounded him, that she'd hurt herself, she had to prove to him…to them…that she wasn't a coward. She'd loved him once. Maybe she loved him again.

Awkward as a teen with her first intimate kiss, she slanted her mouth against his, opened her lips and waited. Waited for him to join her on this new exploration. But he didn't move, didn't offer any help.

Tentatively, she touched her tongue to his lips and she heard a low, erotic growl in the base of his throat. "Is that the best you can do?"

Determination battled the fear inside her. Cupping the back of his neck, feeling the wisps of his hair against her fingers, she pulled him closer, tested the line of his mouth again with the tip of her tongue, and it gave way. Suddenly their tongues met, flesh against flesh, melding, luxuriating in the tastes and textures of each other.

Stunned by her own boldness, by the wild sensations coursing through her, she started to pull away, ready to bolt out of the car and race for her sister's front door, never looking back, never able to face Brody again. As her courage slipped, he took control. His arms came around her, enfolding her in his embrace, which both thrilled and unnerved her. His mouth pressed hard and urgent against her, grinding, opening, invading. She gave. He took.

Her breasts pressed against his chest. Her nipples hardened, tingled with the need for his touch. His hands roamed her back, exploring, searching, molding her to him. Resistance and restraint that she had always experienced with James never surfaced. With Brody she felt free. Free to feel all he aroused in her.

She felt herself falling, tumbling into something she couldn't see, couldn't understand, losing control, losing herself. Was it into love? Or oblivion? Where she'd lose her very soul?

"Brody..." She put a shaky hand to his chest. He nuzzled her neck, sending electric shocks down her spine, making her skin tingle. "I'm..." Her heart pounded with excitement. With fear. "I'm scared."

He stilled. Slowly he pulled away from her, his arms around her, holding her as if he wouldn't ever let her go again. He looked down at her, his eyes smoky with passion. "Of me?"

"Yes..." She shook her head. "N-no. I don't know. Of what you do to me."

He cupped her chin and kissed her lightly, touching his mouth to each corner of her mouth, then running his tongue along her bottom lip, eliciting a wild mixture of sensations through her.

"Brody," she said, breathless. "I—"

"You don't have to be afraid of me, love." His voice sounded ragged. She felt a trembling in his chest. "I won't hurt you."

"It's not you. It's..." A hard lump formed in her throat.

"I know." He smoothed his hand over her hair, sifting his fingers through the strands. "It's okay." He kissed her temple, her forehead, her hair. Her stomach turned inside out. "It's you standing between us. It's always been you. From the beginning. Not some other woman. Not some other man. It's been your fears."

He understood her far better than she understood herself. It unnerved her and at the same time comforted her. Confused, she straightened, edging away from him. She needed time, space. She had to think. And being in Brody's arms she couldn't think clearly or rationally. Or maybe the opposite was true.

When she was in his arms, with him kissing her, everything seemed easy, perfectly clear. When anything separated them, things became muddled and her fears assaulted her.

He settled back into the driver's seat. But his gaze never left hers. She wanted to look away, to try to compose herself, but his eyes acted like a magnet to her heart. "You're afraid of the past. Of yourself."

He reached over and clasped her hand, entwining his fingers with hers. She looked at their joined hands, the shadows playing along their skin, and she couldn't tell where he began and she ended. They were one.

"Take all the time you need," he said, his voice soft but confident. "I can wait. I've waited this long for you. I can wait until you're ready."

"What if that day never comes?" Her voice trembled with suppressed emotions.

"It will." He spoke the words as a promise.

It was simply a matter of time. How much time depended on her. She began to wonder if second chances were possible.

Eleven

"Is there anyone who has any reason why these two should not be wed?" the minister asked. He peered out over the congregation gathered beneath the virginal white tent set up along the back side of the Double Crown's sprawling adobe-style estate.

Brody sat among his family with Jillian right beside him. He didn't expect anyone to protest the wedding of his brother Reed and bride, Mallory. After all, it was obvious to everyone how the two adored each other. But Brody had plenty of doubts and questions regarding his own heart's eagerness to suddenly commit to Jillian.

What had gotten into him?

Why on earth had he said it was only a matter of time before the two of them made love? Had he lost his mind? Or his heart?

And what would happen after they made love? Would marriage automatically follow?

His intentions toward Jillian were as clear as the U.S. tax codes. Never in his life had he been so uncertain, so sure and tentative at the same time, with himself or with a woman. He cursed the emotions pouring out of his heart, cursed the questions, his hesitancy. But he couldn't deny it, either.

Yes, he wanted her. God, the desire was stronger

than the constant, unrelenting pull of gravity. He needed her. Needed her as he needed air to breathe.

Watching her this past week at work as she went about mundane tasks of filing and typing on the computer, he became entranced, mesmerized by each tiny movement—the tilt of her chin, the way her hand hooked a lock of blond hair behind her delicate ear, her quick, unguarded smile. After years of feeling a gaping hole ache in his chest, he knew only Jillian had the ability to make him complete again.

But stark, cold fear kept him from allowing what seemed so natural between them from happening, from coming full circle.

Sitting beside her at his brother's wedding beneath the awning of the shimmering white tent, hearing the somber strands of the violins, watching the ceremony unfold in front of the cluster of family and friends gathered, Brody wondered if he could let himself love Jillian again. His heart pounded ''Yes!'' with each steady beat. Could he marry her? His mind shouted ''No!'' with each resonant question that battered his brain.

Dressed in a lemony-colored suit, with her ankles demurely crossed and her hands tightly clasped in her lap, Jillian seemed caught up in the celebration of love and romance. Brody wondered what her and James's wedding had been like. Had it fulfilled all her girlhood fantasies? Had she worn a Cinderella wedding dress, full and glittery? Or a sleek, mature dress giving a bold glimpse of her feminine curves? Had she given James a chaste kiss or an intimate, lingering one full of promise and purpose?

Once again, like a stinging slap, he faced the fact

that he had not been the first man in Jillian's life…or bed. Not that he thought he had to marry a virgin. But he was the only man for Jillian. Resentment wrenched his insides that someone else had claimed her first.

Even though he knew her marriage to James had been painful, Brody couldn't escape the haunting truth that she'd married James of her own free will. She'd said as much herself.

Feeling his hands clench with unmitigated jealousy, he turned his attention to the bride and groom as they exchanged vows. Mallory's voice wafted soft and sweet through the congregation. Reed sounded sure and confident in his love. And Brody knew he couldn't take a similar profound step until he felt the same.

Having never paid much attention to weddings when his friends or relatives had tied the knot, he found his focus sharp, his senses heightened, as new awareness and interest took hold today. He noticed each tiny detail from the sheer lace sleeves of Mallory's wedding dress to the white satin bows lining the center aisle. In spite of the fans set up around the periphery of the oversize tent and a soft summery breeze filtering through, heat nettled him. Suddenly the fragrance of jasmine and gardenias mingled with Jillian's carefree floral perfume and felt cloying, suffocating to him.

Brody watched Mallory give Reed a watery smile as he slipped a glittering diamond band on her left hand. His brother's Adam's apple jerked with suppressed emotions. Beside him, Jillian dabbed her eyes with a linen handkerchief. An overwhelming sense of possessiveness surged inside him, swelling into a need to shelter and protect her. But did he want the responsibility of till death did they part?

Uncomfortable emotions wrestled inside him, pummelled him with guilt and longing. Fearful questions shadowed his heart, creeping up from behind and dragging him down into a mire of doubt.

"I now pronounce this couple husband and wife." The minister finished the ceremony. With a nod to the groom, he added, "You may kiss the bride."

With love and awe shining in his eyes, Reed cupped Mallory's jaw and gave her a kiss that left no doubts that this was his wife, his woman forever and ever.

Brody felt his insides tighten as his senses magnified on Jillian sitting beside him. The need to kiss her, hold her, make love to her overwhelmed him. But would she let him? Would she trust him again? He knew without that basic trust they had no future. Feeling all those doubts and questions clamp around him like chains, could he with a clear conscience make love to her?

After the bride and groom swept down the center aisle with the crowd clapping and the violins playing, Jillian turned to Brody, her hand on his arm, making his skin overheat. "That was beautiful." Tears shimmered in her turquoise eyes, reminding him of the Coral Sea back home. "They seem so happy."

He nodded, unable to speak.

Gathering her purse, she asked, "Where will the reception be?"

"In the courtyard."

As the rows of family and friends filed out of the

tent and ambled toward the inner sanctuary held within the sandstone walls of the Double Crown adobe-style house, Brody took Jillian's arm. She felt delicate and small, but the tilt of her chin reminded him of her strength of character. Pride that she was beside him at this family occasion surged inside him.

The courtyard had been decorated with yellow and red bougainvillea, lush ferns and climbing ivy. All with Mallory's decorative touch. Already the bride and groom were posing for pictures beneath an archway of greenery and white rosebuds before moving to stand beside the five-tiered wedding cake. Curled shavings of white chocolate swirled over the sugary frosting. Brody had never realized so much went into a wedding and again he thought of Jillian's first marriage and all the preparations she must have orchestrated. On her own. Without her mother's help.

Servers wearing black slacks and white shirts handed out champagne-filled crystal flutes to the guests. A slight woman with mousy brown hair pulled back into a bun walked up to Brody and Jillian. "Want some champagne?"

Brody took one glass off the tray and thanked the woman. "What's your name?"

"Betsy, sir," she answered.

"Betsy, the lady here needs a glass of..." Brody paused and glanced at Jillian. "What would you like, love? Ginger ale?"

She gave him a warm smile that filed down the jagged edges of his heart. "That would be fine."

"Ginger ale, then," he told the server.

"Yes, sir. I'll be right back."

Taking a sip of the champagne, Brody couldn't

keep from asking the haunting question. "Does this make you think of your wedding?"

Startled, Jillian's eyes widened. She gave a half-hearted laugh. "Not exactly."

He cursed himself for asking. It probably brought her pain just remembering James.

Her gaze swept over the courtyard and mingling guests and settled on the bride and groom who had their arms around each other. "Reed and Mallory seem to truly love each other. You know," she tilted her face toward the warm glow of the setting sun, "I had this sinking feeling when I said 'I do' that it was a mistake." She took a deep breath and placed her hand on her abdomen as if at peace now. "And our wedding was…well, James decided on everything. Where the wedding would take place, when. He wanted the bridesmaids to wear black. He thought it made them look more sophisticated. He chose the wedding cake, the hors d'oeuvres, even my dress."

"Why?" he asked, not sure if he was more surprised that Jillian wouldn't stand up for herself or that she apparently hadn't loved James as he'd imagined.

She gave a slight shrug. "I couldn't complain. He paid for everything. Or his father did." She looped a lock of blond hair behind her ear. "I've told you how poor I was growing up. My mother wasn't hoarding money under her mattress. After I paid off her hospital and funeral expenses, I didn't have much left."

He imagined how quickly she'd had to grow up, to take control of her mother's finances, limited though they were, and handle everything. "What about your sister?"

"She was already married. In a bad marriage of

her own, actually. So she had her own worries. I told her I'd take care of things.''

His heart ached for her.

"Anyway, James offered to pay for the wedding. So it would be in the style he was accustomed to. He did like to spend money. Most of the time it was other people's money. And he wasn't very good about paying back loans.''

His brows slanted downward. His shoulders tightened. "Did he leave you in debt?''

She nodded, her lips compressed. "The house didn't belong to us, anyway. His father owned it. But I didn't feel right staying there. That's when I came to live with my sister in San Antonio. I suppose I could have declared bankruptcy, but that didn't seem right to leave all the people he owed in the lurch. So I used what little insurance money I received after his death to pay everything off.''

Awed by her strength, her resilience, her integrity, he felt pride swell inside him. Regret lodged in his throat. He wished he could have been there for her. To help her. But she was right. She'd done okay on her own. Without anyone. Without him.

More doubts swirled inside his head. Would she ever need him?

She placed her hand on his arm as if to reassure him. But it only stirred deep longings inside him. "Don't worry. I'm okay. It was like starting with a clean slate.''

Not sure what to say, how to respond, how to broach the question making him feel stiff-kneed, Brody nodded toward the round lace-skirted tables. "Would you like to get something to eat?''

"All right."

Together they filled their plates with smoked salmon rosettes on crisp rye toast, mushroom caps filled with crabmeat, and fresh blueberries and strawberries dipped in whipped cream, brown sugar and chocolate Grand Marnier sauce.

"Mmm," she murmured biting into a juicy strawberry, "the food is delicious."

Brody couldn't take his gaze off the dollop of whipped cream clinging to her bottom lip. Unable to stop himself, he caught it with the edge of his thumb. Tiny sparks erupted along his spine as he met her electric blue-green eyes. Could she feel the desire, too? Did she need him the way he needed her?

"Harrumph!" A gruff voice snuffed out the sizzle between Jillian and Brody. "Son, are you going to introduce me to this lovely lady?"

Jillian dabbed her mouth with a turquoise napkin.

"My pleasure, Dad." Brody met his father's smiling gray eyes, the only physical similarity between his father and himself. He put a hand at Jillian's lower back. "Jillian Hart...Tanner, this is my father, Teddy Fortune. Dad, Jillie and I went to Winslow College together."

"Well, I'll be." Teddy chuckled. Sunlight glinted off the silver strands shooting through his blond hair. "You don't sound like you're from Down Under."

"No, sir," she said, shaking the older gentleman's hand. "I'm a Texan."

"Well, my brother Ryan says there aren't any prettier women than here in Texas. I have to admit I disputed that fact, for the sake of my lovely wife, Fiona, and daughter, Matilda, but you, my dear, make me think he's right.''

She smiled. "So this is where Brody gets his charm.''

Teddy clapped his son on the back. "Bring this lady around more often, Son. She's a keeper.''

Brody had to agree. But watching his father walk away and stop to chat with Griff, he couldn't escape the underlying reason for his fears—Jillian's unborn child.

"Your father and his brother were recently reunited, is that right?'' Jillian asked.

He assumed she'd heard the rumors at work like everyone else and gave a crisp nod before gulping more of the chilled champagne.

"Had they been apart for a long while?'' she asked.

"Their whole lives. They'd never even met. Josiah Talbot kidnapped my father when he was a baby,'' Brody explained.

"Kidnapped?''

"Yeah, my great-grandfather hated his son-in-law, Kingston Fortune. Said he stole his daughter, Patience. Actually they did sneak off to get married. Then Kingston was shipped off to fight in the Second World War. While in Europe, his wife, Patience, who was my grandmother, died during childbirth. Instead of contacting Kingston about his newborn son, Josiah took off with Teddy. Took him to New South Wales to raise him. That's how we all ended up in Oz…Australia.''

It struck Brody then why Jillian's baby put a barrier between him and a resolute commitment. Not only had his father suffered during his childhood being raised by a tyrannical Josiah, but Brody's brother, Griff, had endured an equally terrible ordeal as a child. One he never had shared with the Fortunes. Griff had never totally accepted their generosity. He was a loner.

Now, Brody worried what the outcome of raising a child that wasn't his would be. He imagined what it would be like to hold James's baby, to care for it, to raise it. To try to love it. Would he always see the pain James had caused Jillian? Would he resent the baby as much as he resented the fact that James had been the first man in Jillian's life?

He didn't know the answers to his burning questions. He wasn't sure he wanted to look deep enough to discover his dark, unforgiving side. But he knew conditional love wouldn't be fair. To Jillian. Or the baby.

And would condemn any marriage to failure.

The bridal couple began their first dance as man and wife. Their bodies moved fluidly as one, the bride's handkerchief skirt swishing around her long, lithe legs. Their hands blended together. Their smiles melted into a united kiss. The music swirled and dipped. It became hard to distinguish if the music or the couple was leading. Jillian felt a lump of longing form in her throat.

Her gaze inadvertently shifted toward Brody. The deepening tones of sunlight glinted off his black hair, giving it the shine of split coal. Dressed in a marble-gray suit that matched his eyes, he wore a butter-cream-colored tie. The expensive suit fabric moved over his chiseled muscles with the fluidity of a smoky mist, stirring hot images inside her head, making her remember what he'd said to her only a week ago.

Take all the time you need. I can wait. I've waited this long for you. I can wait until you're ready. His voice had radiated in her head, burned her with his truth, his desire. Heat shimmered off her skin in tiny waves.

Desperate to gain control of her faculties and her resistance, which she felt slipping each time she looked at him, she sipped the glass of cool ginger ale and averted her gaze. Brody stood so close to her she could feel his warmth, his interest as strong and glaring as the sun's red and orange rays as it dipped toward the horizon.

No matter how hard she tried, she couldn't divert her thoughts away from him. His musky scent saturated her senses. His bold glances and broad shoulders stirred emotions and longings she'd long ago forgotten she possessed. His warm, melodic voice as he whispered in her ear, making sure she had everything she needed, sent tiny shivers down her spine and made her wish for things she had no right to hope for.

"Here you are!" Matilda declared as she sidled up to them, a glass of champagne in one hand and a plate of cake in the other. "Wasn't the wedding dreamy?"

Jillian nodded, grateful for the interruption. "Beautiful."

"I'd say Reed's lost what little sense he once had." Brody's sudden smile gave his words the right tint of humor.

"You don't have a romantic bone in your body." Matilda set her plate on a nearby table and batted the back of her hand against his arm. "No wonder you couldn't keep Jillian when you had her."

Brody's gaze sharpened but he remained silent, brooding. All Jillian could hear was the thud-thud-thud of her heart battering her chest. Lack of romance hadn't been the problem between them. He'd always been too charming, too persuasive. Was she falling for the same old line again?

Now that they knew what had transpired between them, torn them apart, now that Brody had refuted Gail's version, Jillian wondered if they couldn't pick up where they had left off ten years ago. Or was that foolhardy?

Oblivious of her fumbling statement, Matilda turned to a woman trailing after her. "I wanted to introduce you to Dr. Willa Simms. This is my unromantic brother, Brody. And his assistant, Jillian Tanner."

The woman with slate-blue eyes and wavy auburn hair gave them a pleasant but reserved smile.

"Doctor?" Brody asked.

"Purely academic," she said, shaking his hand.

"She has her Ph.D. in political science," Matilda added. "A real brainer."

"I suppose I'll be seeing you often," Willa said, "while I'm staying at the Double Crown."

"Oh?" Brody quirked an eyebrow.

"Willa is Uncle Ryan's godchild," Matilda explained. "She's going to be teaching at Texas A&M University this fall and is waiting for her apartment in College Station to be redecorated. Until then she's all ours. So we'll have to make her feel welcome."

"Oh, you already have." An embarrassed hue

brightened the petite woman's delicate features. "The Fortunes have been very generous with their hospitality."

"Watch out for my sister, though," Brody said, smiling. "She'll set you up with every cowboy between here and the Red River if you're not careful."

Matilda nudged her big brother with her elbow. "Can I help it if I believe in love? Maybe I'll bring Willa to San Antonio for a wild weekend at your place. Jillian, you'll have to go out with us."

Brody frowned. Jillian wasn't sure if he resented his sister's intrusion or worried about Matilda's penchant for fun.

"San Antonio is where Brody's been spending more and more time lately." Matilda pouted, as if irritated that she hadn't seen enough of her big brother. "You rarely come out to the Double Crown for weekends anymore."

"I've been busy," he explained. His gaze slanted toward Jillian. "With this merger."

Even though the temperature dipped slightly as evening turned to night, an intense heat burrowed within her. His warning that it was only a matter of time before they took their relationship further echoed inside her head and rattled her composure. Was she ready? Was he? Did he only want her? Or could he love her as well as her baby?

Her desire battled her fears. Need swelled inside her, like a wave crashing over her, consuming her. She wanted Brody with all her heart. But those desires had almost killed her a few years back. What if she was making another mistake? She'd made so many.

How could she tell if this was a smart move or a fatal error? How could she trust her own instincts?

"How are you feeling?" Matilda asked, turning her attention on Jillian.

"Fine, thanks." She felt the gazes of the others in the twinkling candlelight focus on her and her insides shifted uncomfortably.

"Jillian's pregnant," Matilda explained to Willa.

"Matilda," Brody admonished.

"It's all right." Jillian put a hand on his arm and felt the tension ripple along his muscles. "I don't mind others knowing…not now…not anymore." Not since he'd learned her secret. After all, soon nothing would hide the obvious, not even the flared waists of her suits.

"Congratulations," Willa said. "How wonderful."

"Isn't it?" Matilda beamed. "I think being pregnant would be the most exciting experience. I envy you."

Jillian didn't doubt Brody's younger sister's words but she wondered what logic the young woman was using. After all, Jillian was a single woman, without a husband, without a family to support her. It was not an ideal situation that she would have readily planned. But she also couldn't resent her baby. After the pain and suddenness of James's death and her financial straits, being pregnant had buoyed her spirits. Her baby was the one thing in her life that gave her hope and pride.

Then she noticed Brody's deepening frown as he stared at his sister, as if struck dumb by her comment on being jealous of Jillian's pregnancy.

"Well, come on, Willa," Matilda said, picking up

her plate of cake and giving a couple of hip thrusts to the lively salsa music the band was playing. "I want to introduce you to some others over here. Maybe we can stir up some action...or at least some dancing partners."

"It was nice to meet you two," Willa said as she followed the brash young Fortune woman.

Brody gulped the rest of his champagne. A smile tugged at Jillian as she watched concern consume him. His overprotectiveness endeared him to her even more. Watching him today with his family, seeing the way he accepted his new cousins and loved and respected Griff, Jillian began to think Brody might be the perfect man for her, as a husband, and for her baby, as a daddy.

"I'm sure she didn't mean what she said." Jillian offered the only words of comfort she could think of as sparkling lights surrounding the courtyard were switched on. The tiny white lights winked and blinked like stars, accentuating the flickering candlelight from the tables.

"You mean, about wanting to be pregnant?"

"That, and envying me." She gave a coarse chuckle. "What's there to envy?"

His gaze softened on her, and her pulse quickened. "Everything."

"Did I hear Matilda right, what she said?" Griff Fortune stepped up to them, his frown matching Brody's.

"Let the woman alone." Dawson Prescott, the top financial analyst at Fortune TX, Ltd., moved in between Griff and Brody.

"Woman?" Griff looked astonished. "Why, she's only a kid."

Brody managed a harsh laugh. "You heard right." He reached for another flute of champagne off of a passing waiter's tray. He handed Griff and Dawson their own glasses. "Think we could hire twenty-four-hour-a-day guards for Matilda?"

"Not a bad idea," Griff said, his gaze narrowing on his little sister across the room. "I'll look into it. Who's that pretty woman hanging out with her?"

"A guest of Uncle Ryan's. Seems harmless."

Griff snorted. "You can't be too careful. Not with Clint Lockhart still on the loose."

"You two are impossible." Jillian laughed. "Leave Matilda alone."

"She's a grown woman, for Pete's sake," Dawson added, his gaze more appreciative of Matilda's curves than either brother would have liked.

"Who's Pete?" Griff asked, tipping his champagne glass to his lips.

Dawson laughed, his hazel eyes sparkling. "Guess I said the wrong thing."

"Never mind." Jillian shook her head with dismay. "Don't worry about them. They're just being over-protective big brothers."

"I'd imagine Matilda might call it something else." Dawson took a bite of cake.

"A nuisance," Jillian added with a nod.

Brody scowled. "We've got to do something about her."

"There's nothing you can do," Dawson said. "Believe me, my half sister just married your brother. Trust me on this. When it's time, little sisters are going to do what they want. You can't stop it. Especially when they fall in love.''

"Like hell," Brody said.

"You're no help these days," Griff complained. "Seeing you're so busy with…the merger." His narrowing gaze on Jillian told her he knew something besides mergers and acquisitions was taking place in their San Antonio offices. Turning to Dawson, he cornered his friend. "You have to help."

"With what?"

"Keeping an eye on Matilda," Brody clarified.

"You're nuts." Dawson took another bite of cake.

"Desperate," Griff supplied. "Will you do it?"

Dawson shrugged. "Sure. I guess. If I see her around, I'll keep an eye out for her. But I doubt I'll be seeing much of her. With her staying here at the ranch. But if she comes my way, then I'm your man."

"She says she wants to come back for a visit in San Antonio," Brody added.

"You men!" Jillian laughed. "You're all so arrogant. If a woman is going to fall in love, there's nothing that can stop her."

Brody's gaze focused on her. "Tell me more."

"You know," Dawson said, "if I had a lady as beautiful as Jillian standing beside me, I wouldn't be concentrating on my little sister. I'd be off dancing."

Brody gave Jillian a smile that could have melted Antarctica. "Right. Not a bad idea." He took Jillian's glass of ginger ale and handed it to his business associate along with his own. "If you'll excuse us…"

Whisking her into his arms, he moved her onto the dance floor stationed in the middle of the courtyard.

His arms were strong and demanding, his embrace as warm and intoxicating as the night breeze.

"Prescott was right," he said, his voice deep and resonant.

"About what?"

"This is much better," he said, whispering in her ear, his voice rolling over her like warm water.

Her nerves knocked together like her knees. She tried to sort through her jumbled thoughts. It was one thing to stand next to Brody and try to suppress her desire. It was quite another to be in his arms, feel his hand on her waist, be but a kiss away from him. "Better than plotting a strategy against your little sister?"

"Not against," he protested. He tugged her closer and breathed in the scent of her hair. "What sister?"

Tilting her head upward, she gave him a smile. "You're something, you know?"

"Only when I'm with you." Quickening his step, he maneuvered her around a thickening band of dancers.

She felt the music flow over them, sweeping them into a world where only she existed with Brody. A world of starlight and candlelight. The surrounding darkness swallowed the wedding party and curious family and friends into the shadows. Jillian's desire struck like a flame, burning her with the touch of his hand, the warmth of his breath on her cheek, the solid heat of his chest and sturdy shoulder. Her stomach did a slow roll as if the sun were tumbling out of the sky.

This time, she couldn't blame the sensations stirring inside her on the baby.

She wasn't sure if she wanted to kiss him or push

him away. Her heart knew the answer that her body had been trying to beat into her head. She wanted Brody, needed him more than she'd ever desired any man. The years and distance between them hadn't dulled his powerful, shattering effect on her. And she knew his words were correct. It was only a matter of time before she fell hard.

Why was she fighting him? Why was she fighting herself?

Holding on to him as they swayed together to the romantic music pulsing around them, she thought of Brody and his extended family. He readily accepted and felt only respect and love for his uncle Ryan and the Texas Fortunes. He treated Griff as his real, flesh-and-blood brother, even though she knew Griff had been adopted. Her heart began pounding out the truth.

If Brody could accept his family so easily with all its idiosyncrasies, then maybe he could accept her baby as his own. Maybe, just maybe, there was a future waiting for them. It was simply waiting for her to realize and accept.

As the final chords of the romantic song drawled like an east Texas accent, Brody dipped his head and claimed her mouth. His lips were gentle yet demanding, urgent but patient. Her pulse fluttered, and her heart took flight. As her senses swirled, she put an unsteady hand on his chest. In spite of the chaotic sensations tumbling through her, he made her feel steady, secure, safe. It was a heady excitement she couldn't remember experiencing. Only Brody made her world stop spinning, and at the same time sent her into orbit.

"Brody," she said, arching away from him but not daring to leave his embrace.

"Hmm?" He nuzzled her neck as the next song began. This tune was livelier, but Brody maintained a slow, erotic pace as if he were making love to her rather than dancing.

Suddenly she wanted to be closer to him, closer than prudence allowed in this setting. She needed to feel his arms around her, taste his kisses until she couldn't feel or think. She wanted all the doubts and strife that had built between them to melt away.

Knowing this was either the smartest or dumbest decision she'd ever make, trusting the unsteady beat of her heart more than she probably should, she curled her fingers along the back of his neck, feeling the tapering of his hair, the coarse texture against her sensitized flesh.

"Take me home," she whispered.

Immediately he lifted his head and stared down at her. "Are you ill?"

She shook her head and stared into the warmth of his gray eyes. No, she was simply head over heels in love. And no longer willing to deny it, him, or herself. "I need... Brody, please, just take me home."

The corner of his mouth pulled into a half smile that tightened her stomach. He gave her a solid, reassuring kiss as an answer, and clasped her hand in his. "Anything you want, love."

Twelve

"**G**et in the car. Quick!"

It was well past midnight and the night sky looked like a black hole absorbing all light. If Clint had bothered to take a closer look he would have noticed the dark gray clouds blocking out the stars and passing over the moon. Instead he only noticed shadows creeping along the adobe walls of the Double Crown's entrance gate. His nerves felt brittle.

"Hurry," he said in a shouted whisper as he once again shot a look over his shoulder, half expecting to see the flashing red and blue lights of a police cruiser.

Betsy looked weary and well-used, like a crumpled napkin, with faded lipstick and wrinkles at the corners of her eyes deeper than when she'd left early that afternoon to work on the Fortune wedding. She plopped into the passenger seat and tugged on the heavy door, but it stuck. Reaching across her slim frame, he yanked it shut. He flinched at the grating sound of the door's rusty hinges.

She pursed her lips to kiss him but he didn't have time. Or the desire.

"What the hell kept you?" he snapped, shoving the Ford's shift into drive. Stepping on the gas pedal, he heard the spitting of gravel as he swerved onto the

narrow two-lane highway leading away from the Fortune ranch.

"I had to stay and clean up after the wedding couple left. I couldn't leave before the guests. You didn't
want me to get fired, did you?"

"It doesn't matter anymore."

"Has something happened?"

"No." Not yet, anyway. He gave her a cursory
glance and saw the hurt in her drab blue eyes. Reaching across the cracked seat, he took her hand in his,
felt the chafed skin, the nervous sweat. Had he pushed
her too far? He couldn't chance losing her devotion.
Not yet anyway. Not until he was far away from the
Double Crown, Leather Bucket and San Antonio. Not
until he was across the Mexican border. "Sorry I'm
jumpy."

She clasped his hand tighter. "It's okay. I understand. I'm the one that should be sorry." She pulled
his hand to her lap, laying his palm flat against her
skinny thigh, and stroked his fingers. "I shouldn't
have been so late."

"It's okay, sugar," he said, softening his voice,
feeling the tension in his shoulders ease as the miles
between him and the Double Crown multiplied. The
breeze from the open windows slapped at him. "Let's
go home."

She looped her arm through his in a silent promise
of passion. He had to give her credit. She was adven-
turous, willing to do most anything he asked…in bed
or anyplace else. And she was always eager.

The clankety-clank of the oil pan made his hand
tighten on the steering wheel. Tonight he'd decided

to steal another car as soon as everything came together. Betsy's Ford wouldn't do for his getaway.

"What did you learn tonight, sugar? Anything good?" He rubbed her thigh, pulling her skirt high on her leg, teasing her. God, sometimes he thought he could just about make her purr.

Leaning her head back on the seat, she sighed with pleasure. "It was hard learning all those Fortunes' names. There's so many of them. I guess the really big news, besides the wedding, was that Ryan Fortune's goddaughter—Willa something—is living on the ranch. She's a professor or something. Gonna teach at Texas A&M. Must be awfully smart."

"What else?" He moved his hand higher.

"And then there's the Fortunes visiting from Australia." Her voice trembled with desire and need. "Oh, I could listen to those accents forever."

Irritation jabbed at him. "What the hell is wrong with a Texas accent?"

Her eyes snapped open. "Nothin'. Nothin' at all, honey. There's nothin' I like better than your voice, Clint. You make me wild."

"Good. Now go on."

"Well, then there's the gossip about Brody Fortune. He's here working on something for the two companies. I couldn't figure out what. Anyway, he brought his assistant with him. A real pretty gal. And she's pregnant! It was obvious to everybody that a little hanky-panky has been going on in that office."

Clint chuckled.

"Maybe we can fool around ourselves when we get home," she said suggestively.

"Whatever you want, sugar."

She scooted across the seat to snuggle beside him. Her hand eased up the length of his thigh along his faded jeans. Then she stopped, shifted on the bench seat and pulled his fake ID out from under her. "What's this?"

The hair along the back of his neck raised. He shrugged as if it didn't matter. "You got it out of my cabin. Don't you remember, sugar?"

"Yeah, but I didn't leave your ID here in the car. It makes me nervous." She clasped his hand, holding on to him tight, as if he might vanish in front of her eyes. "I worry I'm gonna wake up one mornin' and you're gonna be gone."

He would be. But she didn't have to know that. Not till he was gone.

"Nothin' for you to worry about, sugar. When the time comes…after I get even with Ryan Fortune, then we'll leave. Together." He shifted, hooking his arm around her narrow shoulders. "Now, there's one more thing I need you to do for me. Are you willing?"

She kissed his neck, and the point of her tongue drew a moist line to his ear. "You know I'd do anything for you, Clint."

Brody could hear the blood pumping in his ears and felt it course through his body at a rapid pace. He wanted to take Jillian to his home, his apartment, his bed. But as she had asked, he drove toward her sister's house, unsure how the evening would end.

She'd been giving him shy signals that she was ready to take the next step. But maybe it was his own desire clouding his better judgment. Maybe she was simply tired and wanted to go home. Or maybe she was nervous and didn't want to stay at the wedding.

Whatever she wanted, he would give her. He would take care of her. It was an undeniable need.

The question now was how would he accomplish that? From afar? As a friend? Or as something more, with the intimacy that he yearned for?

His rental car's headlights slashed through the darkness. Only the sound of their breathing filled the interior. With her hand in his, her warm, moist palm against his, her delicate fingers entwined with his, he had a difficult time concentrating on his driving, much less the ramifications of his actions. All he could focus on was her soft fragrance that reminded him of a summery ocean breeze and the feel of her smooth, silky skin against his.

When he paused at a stoplight near her sister's home, he had an urge to run the light. The streets were deserted. What harm could it do? He needed the answer to the simmering question—was she ready or not? But he waited, unwilling to risk her safety.

A few minutes later he pulled up in front of her sister's house and parked, switched off the headlights and cut the engine. He took a deep, steadying breath and said, "I'll get your door."

He helped her out of the low-slung sports car. When she stood, they were but a breath apart. He wanted to dip his head, to taste her lips once more, to test and tease. But if she wanted him, wanted him as much as he needed her, then it was her move, her decision. He wouldn't push or tempt her. Even if the restraint required killed him.

The walk up the sidewalk to the front porch seemed

as long and as arduous as setting out across the Out-back on foot. Night sounds surged around him. Crickets chirped. Fireflies flickered. A dog barked in the distance. Jillian's heels clicked against the concrete walkway. Her hand brushed his, and he felt his skin contract with desire. They stepped around a pumpkin someone had carved and set on the front stoop, and entered the halo of the porch light.

"Well," he said, his voice sticking in his throat like glue.

"Well," she repeated.

The awkward silence tripped between them.

"I suppose I'll see you on Monday," he said, "at the office."

A strange light glinted in her eyes and she tilted her head to the side, staring up at him with what he only imagined was longing. But he was probably mistaken.

"Brody," she said, her voice soft as the fall breeze rustling the leaves covering the lawn. "I... My sister is out of town."

Was she scared about entering the house by herself? Staying alone? It would push him beyond his limit if she wanted him to sleep in another room like a guard dog for protection and companionship.

"You'll be fine." He took a step back, angling himself toward the stairs. He had to go now, before he did something he would regret.

"Brody..." She reached out and touched his hand. Her feathery caress stirred something inside him that he could only label as uncontrollable desire. "Don't go."

"Jillie... What are you saying?" His heart stumbled.

This time her touch was bolder. She took his hand and tugged him closer. "I thought you understood."

"That I want you? That you're driving me crazy?"

She smiled then, but her eyes remained wide and luminous in the moonlight, like deep dark oceans. "Good. Because I feel the same way."

Her words blocked out the last of his rational thoughts. The next thing he knew, they were kissing and fumbling with the lock, stumbling inside. Their breaths hot, their hands urgent, their mouths greedy. All questions and doubts faded beyond his need for Jillian.

She gave a sly, confident smile to the building manager. "Mr. Fortune will be so appreciative of you letting me into his apartment."

"Well, I don't know." The wiry man looked nervous, unsure as he shifted from foot to foot.

"Trust me." She slipped a nice tip into his hand then. Before he could change his mind or call for security, she closed the door between them, shutting him out of Brody Fortune's luxury apartment. She had to get ready.

She leaned back against the door and took a deep breath, inhaling what she imagined was Brody's cologne. Her nerve endings electrified, trembled with apprehension.

She didn't need the overhead lights to see the money that had been poured into the decorating. Marble and hardwood floors, elaborate molding along the high ceilings, silver accents and rich mahogany woods that reflected the moonlight streaming through the windows had been used in subtle, classy ways. Thick drapes skirted the tall windows that ran from floor to ceiling.

The ticking of a nearby clock alerted her. Although the hour was late, she felt wired, as if she'd had one cup of coffee too many. It wouldn't be long. Brody would be home soon. And she would be waiting.

Waiting for him.

Setting her cumbersome bag on the entry table, she walked through the shadows darkening the apartment. The dim glow of lights along the floorboard lit her way. Expensive furnishings filled each room. She breathed in the scents of leather and lemony furniture polish. Her heart hammered anxiously in her chest.

Meandering through the kitchen, she trailed her finger along the smooth tile countertop, over the rough butcher-block cutting board and along the cool blade of a knife.

Then she entered what she imagined was his study. For a few restless minutes, she sat in a comfortable stuffed chair beside a rolltop desk and imagined Brody sitting here, concentrating on some big business deal, adding more money to his already fat bank account. She smoothed her hands down the arms of the chair over the textured fabric.

Restless, an itchy feeling tingling beneath the surface of her skin, she located his bedroom. Her gaze settled on the wide, expansive bed. Unfolding her body along the satin comforter, she laid her head on Brody's pillow. She wondered what he dreamed about. She felt a ruffle of anticipation in the pit of her stomach. What did he long for in the early morning hours when he hung in a suspended place between sleep and full consciousness?

Soon it wouldn't matter.

Soon he'd have new plans.

Plans involving her.

She imagined his shock and surprise when he discovered her in his bedroom, curled up on his bed. Waiting for him.

Then soon she'd be the bride she'd always imagined.

Jillian felt like a virgin bride.

Jittery, awkward, excited.

Eager, nervous, self-conscious.

Her heartbeat pulsed erratically in her throat. Part of her wanted to crumple inward, withdraw, but Brody's wildly tempting kisses awakened a wanton side of her as they stumbled into her sister's darkened house. It was a side of herself she'd never experienced, never known existed.

She tugged and yanked on his shirt, pulling it loose from his slacks until she could run her hands over his bare back. His muscles were firm, rippled with strength. She felt the hard edge of his shoulder blades and the ridges of his spine as her fingers trailed downward toward his hips. Hot to her touch, his skin burned, branding her with his own inner heat, his own desire.

Urgency radiated off his skin, pulling her in, magnetizing her. Her insides vibrated with need. For the first time in her life she felt out of control sexually, desperate, eager, demanding. As if she had no choice. No resistance.

Maybe that was best. Since none of her decisions over the past few years had been worth a damn. But holding on to Brody, her breasts pressing against his chest with each ragged breath, feeling his hands touching, caressing, stroking, possessing, she knew this was right. Oh, so right. She felt it straight through to her soul.

"Ah, Jillie," he murmured against her ear, his voice deep and penetrating, his breath arousing, his tongue tempting as it swirled along the outer edges of her ear. "This is crazy."

"I know." The pounding of her heart deafened her to any doubts or questions. "Don't stop. Please, don't stop."

Against her mouth, she felt his lips pull into a crooked smile. That smile that had won her heart so long ago. He cupped her face and pressed his forehead to hers. His eyes were dark with desire, his gaze hot with need. "I've waited too long for this moment with you."

"Me, too."

Brody sucked in a harsh breath. He could take her hard and fast. It would end the burning ache inside him. But he knew the pressure, the need, the desire wouldn't disappear entirely. He'd never get enough of her. He wanted more. So much more.

He wanted every part of her to cry out for him. He didn't want this moment, this time with her to end. And if it took all night, it would be worth the delay, the struggle.

"There's no need to rush," he said. "I'm not going anywhere. No reason to hurry." Was he trying to convince himself or her?

Her hips pressed against his groin. "There isn't?"

A moan rumbled deep in his throat. "You're not the woman I used to know."

"Is that bad?" she asked, wariness darkening the blue of her eyes to slate.

He kissed her as if he could absorb her doubts, swallow her uneasiness. "No. You're better than I ever imagined. And I've imagined a lot."

"You have?" she asked, disbelief entering her voice.

He nuzzled her neck and tightened his hold on her, wrapping his arms around her slight frame, feeling the soft fullness of her breasts, the swell of her belly, the dip at the base of her spine. His pulse raced, his blood pumped recklessly.

"What have you imagined?" she asked, a seductive smile curving her lips.

"Let me show you." He slanted his mouth across hers, tested the seam of her lips, tasting, claiming, devouring. With one quick move, he yanked her suit jacket off her shoulders. He crumpled the material in his fists and fought back the urge to take her here, against the front door, in the entryway of her sister's house. "Where's your room?"

"Down the hall." She arched her back, giving him access to her neck, her breasts.

With an open, eager mouth, he kissed the graceful column of her throat, dipping his tongue into the hollow where her pulse throbbed, tasted the saltiness of her skin, breathed in the heady scent of her perfume and raw heat. His mouth made moist marks across the front of her white silk shirt. He released her jacket, let it fall to the floor at their feet, then hooked an arm behind her back and beneath her knees. Lifting her against his chest, he carried her down the hall.

"In here," she said, her voice husky as she indicated a partially open door.

With his shoulder, he pushed the door open and entered a dark bedroom. A yellow circle of light emanated from a night-light and cast a hazy glow across a narrow bed. "It's a twin."

"Is that a problem?" she asked, her body stiffening.

He chuckled low. "Only if you wanted to get some sleep."

"Sleep's not what I had in mind."

"Good." He laid her on top of the bed and felt the springs give as he pressed his knee into the mattress.

Grabbing the back of his collar, he pulled his shirt over his head and dropped it onto a heap on the floor. He leaned forward, letting their mouths touch, nip, savor. She opened to him, and he tasted her sweetness.

With one deft hand, he undid the tiny, delicate buttons down the front of her shirt. Pulling away, he slid onto his side, watched her breasts rise and fall with each breath, sharp intakes, uneven exhales. She trembled as if cold, but he could feel heat rising off her skin.

He eased open the panels of her shirt. The satin covering her breasts was smooth, cool. Her flesh beneath the delicate lace cups was flushed and warm. So warm, he felt himself melting as he palmed her, grazing the pad of his thumb over the stiff, taut peak.

A low moan broke from her parted lips as he

snapped open the clasp between her breasts. Her back arched off the bed and her hands curled into fists.

He skimmed a finger over the curve of her breast, between the deep valley, along the underside until he heard her sharp intake of breath. Smiling down at her, he whispered, "You're beautiful. More beautiful than I remembered."

She felt herself tremble from the inside out. "I'm bigger now," she stated matter-of-factly. "Pregnancy hormones at work."

He traced his finger down the center of her body, between her rib cage, over her belly button, and laid his hand flat against the slight roundness of her stomach. "Will this be okay? We won't hurt the baby?"

Feeling her heart swell with love at his concern, she covered his hand with her own. "It'll be fine."

He lowered his head to her breast, and she felt the moist heat of his mouth on her as his lips pulled and tugged at her nipple. Her breath snagged in her throat.

"It'll be better than fine," he said, his accent rugged and suggestive.

He seduced her with long slow caresses that aroused, demanded, tempted. He kissed her breasts, her abdomen through her skirt. His hand skimmed up along her silk-covered thigh, pushing her skirt higher. With a snap of his fingers, he unhooked her garter. In long, languid strokes, he rolled her stockings down her legs. His tongue traced the curve of her arch. He sucked on her toes, massaged her feet until she felt as if she were floating above the bed like a cloud.

Removing her skirt, he explored every inch of her, running a finger along the elastic band of her lace panties, cupping the aching center of her, dipping his fingers into her moist heat. His caresses quickened. Grew bold. Urgent.

A frenzy built inside her like a storm forming on the horizon, coming closer, closer. His touch set off sparks along her spine. A current raced through her like heat lightning.

Wild and breathless, she clawed at his back, writhed against him, anxious to feel him close, wanting to feel flesh against flesh, his hardness nestled into her softness. A frantic need tore at her mind. Her heart beat rampantly inside her chest.

With shaky hands, she unfastened his slacks, slid them over his narrow hips and he kicked them to the floor. He settled over her, staring down at her, his eyes as stormy and wild as a feverish gust of wind, stirring her to new heights.

"I've waited for this...for you...for a lifetime."

So had she. She felt nervous, delirious.

Easing into her, he watched her, measuring, gauging, appreciating. She felt herself stretch to accommodate him. He filled her completely.

When they were joined, her legs wrapped around him, his arms braced on either side of her head, he kissed her fully, deeply, taking, giving more than she'd ever expected. He started to move slow and steady. She matched his rhythm, urged him faster, bucking beneath him. She palmed his buttocks, her heels pressing into the backs of his thighs.

Pounding shocks of pleasure jolted her. Her body went rigid. Her back arched. Her hands clenched. Her lungs burned. She'd never experienced such intensity, such passion. The climax shattered the last of her composure. She sobbed his name on a ragged breath.

A shuddering rocked her and she clung to him, desperate.

He dipped his face into the curve of her shoulder. His breath was moist and hot on her skin. Her hands moved over his back, felt the unreleased tension in his taut muscles. She lifted his head, looked him in the eye and kissed him. As she plunged her tongue into the depths of his mouth the way he was still deep inside her, she began to rock against him, moving, thrusting, until bodies strained and muscles yearned for release.

With one last thrust, he shuddered. Her name tore from his lips, echoing in the stillness of the room. A tremor started in her belly and spread out to her limbs until she was a quivering mass, helpless and replete. He fit her against his side, in the crook of his arm. His skin was slick with sweat, his breathing coarse and ragged.

With each beat of her heart, she began to believe that Brody was truly the man she'd been meant to love. This was her second chance. One with a bright future. One full of hope and promise. One with Brody always by her side.

Thirteen

Thousands of miles away from Australia and his birthplace, separated from his family and business, Brody had never felt so at home, so right, so complete.

And it was because of Jillian.

With her curled into the crook of his arm, he felt her soft, silky curves along his side, her shapely leg draped over his, her fingers sifting through his chest hair. His body hummed with an awareness he'd never known.

"I thought we'd never be here together," she said, her voice quiet, still with a touch of awe.

He smoothed his hand down her arm, felt the goose bumps rise along her skin. Pulling a blanket up from the end of the bed to cover her, he gave her a tender kiss. "It was more powerful than I ever dreamed."

"For you, too?"

"Honest, love. And you? Did you—" he gave her a sleepy, confident smile as he remembered her abandonment "—enjoy yourself?"

She ducked her head into the side of his neck. "I've never felt anything like that in my life. Ever. It was…" She looked at him then, a smile curving her lips seductively. "Joyous."

He kissed her again, swiftly, completely, then settled her back against his side. Exhaustion settled over him like the warm blanket. He couldn't think of anything better than falling asleep with the woman he loved in his arms. His hand idly caressed the tiny ridges along her spine. This, he decided, was heaven on earth.

One regret pierced his heart. How their lives could have been so different. If only Jillie hadn't believed that ex-girlfriend of his. If only he'd gone after Jillie instead of tending to his wounded pride.

"I have only one regret." The words popped out of his mouth before he considered them more carefully. But then he knew Jillie would understand. Surely she had the same misgivings.

"What's that?" she asked, a tremor entering her voice.

"That I wasn't your first. It should have been me." If not for Gail, it would have been. Then James wouldn't have hurt her with his betrayals and lies. "God, Jillie, imagine how our lives would have been different."

"So different," she echoed. Her hand on his chest stilled.

He could feel her pulse beating in rhythm with his heart. His hand covered the swell of her abdomen. Awestruck, he imagined the tiny life growing inside her. Filled with an incredible sense of responsibility, without the usual pressure, only an intense need to guard and protect both Jillie and her baby, he imagined the pleasure of welcoming this little life into the world, of standing beside Jillian, of supporting her, the baby, of sharing a life with them. Suddenly it seemed insignificant that the child wasn't his.

''And your baby could have been...'' he said, understanding that if things had been different, if he had made love to Jillian ten years ago, if they had married, that they wouldn't have had such personal struggles.

But then they wouldn't have been the same people today. And he wouldn't trade the woman Jillian had become for anything...or anyone. ''Your baby would have been mine.''

Your baby! Your baby? He might as well have said James's baby. For her baby would never—could never be Brody's. Not with his obvious inability to accept it as his own.

Jillian could see the truth now. She understood his regrets, felt them deep in her heart. He wanted her to be a virgin, for him to have been her one and only lover. He wished this child—she covered the soft swell of her belly with her hand—to be his, not James's. She had the same wishes, too. But wishing or regretting couldn't change reality. The ugly fact was that neither she nor her baby were good enough for the likes of Brody Fortune.

What a fool she'd been.

His words spun through her like a cyclone, churning up doubts, plowing through hopes, destroying the dreams she'd begun to imagine possible.

She stared into the darkness folding around them long after she heard his breathing slow and felt his chest rise and fall in a somber cadence of sleep. What now? What would she do now?

She'd made love to her boss. Her boss! What had she been thinking? That was the problem. Brody stole her thoughts with one look, one kiss. Her heart thudded beneath her breast with remorse, sorrow and regret. He'd spoken of regret in the past tense. But she was living it now.

Maybe she could find another job. At least she wasn't showing yet. At least not too much. She only looked as though she'd enjoyed one too many pizzas. So she could make a new start. Again.

She was tempted to sneak out of the bed and leave. But this was her home...or at least where she was living temporarily. Besides, she'd have to face Brody on Monday morning, anyway. What then? Was she a coward?

For too long she'd lived with weakness as if her bones were too brittle, too feeble to stand on their own. It played like a broken record throughout her life. In high school, she'd been so shocked, so grateful, so amazed that the captain of the football team, the most popular boy, the wealthiest boy, had wanted to date her. She'd believed James when he'd told her what a favor he was doing for her.

Even though Brody had been incredibly different, even as the big man on campus, she'd continued to believe that she wasn't good enough, pretty enough or strong enough to keep her man. Believing Gail's lies had given her a degree in self-doubt.

Instead of standing up to Brody and confronting him, she'd run home to her mother, using her mother's sudden illness as a convenient excuse.

Then she'd crawled back to James, heartbroken over her mother's death and Brody's betrayal. What else could she expect or demand from life? She'd tiptoed around James for years. Never challenging his carousing, his drinking, his harsh put-downs.

Why? Why was she always the fool? Why, oh, why, did she feel worthless?

One answer resonated through her entire body—her father. He'd left her mother. He'd deserted their family. He'd abandoned her. And Brody's rejection of her baby stung with the venom of a hornet, poisoning her thoughts and feelings with the ones she'd felt as a child when her father left.

But no more. No more doubting. No more believing that she was unworthy. No more running from confrontations. Her hand closed into a tight, angry fist. Her heart pounded so hard and fast that a headache attacked her temple. "Not this time," she whispered. "This time I'm going to take a stand."

She spent the next hours wondering how she would do that. What would she say? She toyed with words, practiced them in her head. Imagined different responses he might throw at her and how she would respond. By the time light touched the edge of the curtains and he stirred, she felt prepared.

Until he opened those sleepy gray eyes and looked at her, amazement shining in those depths. "You're still here. It wasn't a dream."

"No," she said, softer than she had hoped. Feeling self-conscious and exposed at her state of undress, she edged away from him, as far as she could in the twin bed, and tugged the blankets up over her shoulders.

"Are you cold?" he asked, rubbing her arms with his big hands. She remembered the gentle touch of those hands, the skill, the finesse. The way he'd made her insides explode with passion. Her steely nerve bent under the weight of her need.

"I'm fine."

His brow furrowed as he studied her. "Are you?"

Here was her chance. Blast him with the truth—this could never work. But the words stuck in her throat as the concern in his eyes seemed to punch a hole right through to her soul.

"Sure, why wouldn't I be?"

He leaned up on one elbow. He was too close, crowding her. His sleep-warmed skin made her want to lean toward him. But she resisted the foolish urge. She couldn't give in until she knew exactly where she stood with Brody.

She tried to ignore his disheveled appearance, his bare chest, the dark hairs swirling over his chiseled muscles, the dark shadow covering his square jaw. All of it made him look rumpled and sexy and as harmless as a stuffed teddy bear. Something inside her wanted to curl up next to him, feel his strong arms around her, let his rock-solid chest stabilize her un-balanced world.

But she remembered his words of regret. And her spine stiffened.

He stretched, giving a glance at the clock on the bedside table. His arms tightened around her, pulling her close. He nuzzled her neck. Her skin tingled. "Where did we leave off last night? Don't we have some lost time to make up for?"

"Um, I think I'll take a shower." Maybe if she was clean and dressed she'd feel more sure of herself. She could find the solid footing she needed to con-front him. They couldn't continue this facade. Not with the way he felt about her baby. Just when she'd thought she'd finally made a good decision, fallen into bed with Brody, then realized it was the worst mistake of her life.

"O-kay." His penetrating gaze tried to read her. He looked disappointed that she hadn't invited him to shower with her.

She diverted her gaze, refusing to see the confusion churning in his eyes. Trapped between the wall and the barrier of his chest, she said, "If you don't mind…"

Without question, he turned and swung his long legs over the side of the bed, stretched the taut muscles of his back, tilting his head this way and that, then stood. Nude, waiting for her.

Keeping her gaze on the blue carpet, she yanked the blanket around her, securing her dignity—or what was left of it—and headed for the bathroom without a backward glance. She couldn't afford to look at him. Couldn't stare at that well-honed body of his, remember the strength, the heat of him against her. Or she might waver. And she couldn't meet his concerned gaze. Or she would fall again. Right back in love with him.

Squaring her shoulders, she promised herself she wouldn't make that mistake again. She'd learned her lesson.

A short while later she emerged from the steamy bathroom dressed in an oversize sweatshirt and shorts. She stopped when she realized her bedroom was vacant. The twin bed, with its rumpled sheets, yawned wide and empty. Her heart tripped over itself. Her gaze darted around the room. His clothes were missing. Where was he? Had *he* left?

Cautiously, she padded barefoot down the hallway.

The potent aroma of coffee warned her before she saw him. He stood at the sink, his back to her, lifting a cup to his mouth.

Early morning sunlight poured through the kitchen windows and shone against his black wavy hair. He hadn't bothered to put on his shirt. But he wore his gray slacks. Thank God.

Here goes, she thought, once again avoiding staring at the way his broad shoulders accented his narrow hips. She cleared her throat. She wouldn't back down this time.

When he faced her, leveling her with those eyes that seemed to search her very soul, she turned toward the coffeemaker and filled a cup.

"At least you didn't add too many grounds this time." She tried to lighten the awkwardness of the morning after.

"I've been practicing." He gave her a smile that she couldn't avoid, that made her heart palpitate. "For you."

Shaken by his ability to tempt her, she veered toward the refrigerator and yanked open the door. A ketchup bottle and Italian dressing container rattled on the door shelf. She stared at the sparse contents. One egg remained in the blue carton. An open can of soda sat on the top shelf all alone, forgotten. A few slices of bread remained of the whole-wheat loaf. "I don't have much to offer in the way of breakfast."

Not that she wanted to feed him. She needed some time alone, to gather her strength, focus her thoughts, figure out what to do, what she wanted. No matter what her body might yearn for, she had her baby to think of first and foremost. She didn't want a man who could love her and not her child.

But she knew then she truly loved him. That's why her heart felt as if a vise squeezed the life out of her.

She heard him moving toward her and braced herself. From behind her, he wrapped his arms around her middle and rested his chin on her shoulder. "I'm not hungry. But I bet you are."

"Not really." The chill of the refrigerator couldn't combat the heat of his body. He jumbled her thoughts with a simple touch. With a brief glance, he could bring her to her knees.

She didn't think she could swallow a bite. But she had to. For the baby's sake. "Maybe, I could make some toast."

"I have an idea," he said, his voice as warm as the scent of coffee.

Her pulse skittered with desire. No, uncertainty. Anger, she decided. But as he nuzzled the side of her neck, tiny shockwaves erupted along her spine, shaking apart her determination.

Push away, she told herself. But God, he felt so good. Too good. Just as Brody was too good to believe, so was love. She spun out of his arms.

But he caught her, trapped her, his hands braced against the wall on either side of her. "What's wrong?"

Tell him, she coached herself. But again the words wouldn't come. Deep hurt resonated in her chest, paralyzing her voice as well as her limbs. Hot, aching tears burned the backs of her eyes.

"Are you okay? Did I hurt you?"

Yes! He'd hurt her desperately. He'd shown her

how love could be, how it could make the earth move beneath your very feet, knock you off balance, destroy you. But he'd also proven to her that love was a fairy tale. One she couldn't believe in anymore.

"Jillie? What's happened?"

Too much.

His hands clasped her shoulders and he hauled her against that wide, solid chest. His mouth slanted across hers before she could protest or even blink. His lips pressured her to respond. Demanded it. And God help her, she did. She opened to him, unable to resist the sweet torture. If he pushed, if he tried to make love to her again, she knew she'd end up on the linoleum, eager, willing, and insane with desire.

Even as her body rejoiced with his intoxicating kiss, her heart crumpled from the harsh pain. She felt stiff and wooden, broken.

When he ended the kiss, he gave her a sexy smile that had once knocked her for a loop. But no more. "That's better."

He wrapped her in his arms, held her against his solid chest. Numb with a cold fear balled up in her stomach, she couldn't find the strength to push him away. His lips nipped at her along the length of her neck, teasing, provoking images she didn't want to remember, stirring desire that she only wanted to forget.

"Here's my idea," he said. "Let's go to my place. I'll catch a quick shower, shave so I don't scrape your skin." His hand rubbed across his jaw, making a rasping sound. His fingers caressed the side of her neck, and she felt a raw ache deep inside.

"That way we'll be gone before your sister gets

home. Didn't you say she was coming back this morning?''

She nodded. She'd forgotten Amy was returning. All she needed was a scene in front of her sister.

"Then," he continued, his voice husky, "we'll have breakfast...and spend the rest of the day in bed."

Her knees felt weak with a need she couldn't understand. Anger pounded in her temples. This wouldn't work. She had to tell him. Now. Before it was too late. But how?

Maybe going to his place would help her find the strength. Maybe it would be easier standing in his living room, rather than her bedroom or her sister's kitchen. After all, once she made her case, she could leave, rather than kick him out of her home. It would be simpler. Cleaner.

Wimp! a tiny voice echoed in her brain.

No. She wasn't a wimp. She was a strategist. Planning the right atmosphere, the perfect time to make a clean break. His apartment would provide that opportunity.

Or would it? Was she simply trying to run away again? Before Brody could? She couldn't make heads or tails of her logic. All she really wanted to do was stay with him forever.

She's nervous, that's all, Brody told himself, putting the key in the lock of his apartment. Jillian stood beside him, squeezing her purse as if it were a neck she was strangling.

Who could blame her for nerves? James had apparently been her first and only lover until Brody. She wasn't used to waking up the morning after making passionate love.

Frankly, he wasn't used to waking up in love, with the woman of his dreams beside him. It had unnerved him, too. And at the same time thrilled him.

"This way, m'lady," he said with a slight bow as he pushed open the door.

She brushed past him into the entryway, her shoulders stiff, her chin tilted at a defensive angle.

"Shall I make coffee?" He gestured toward the kitchen, remembering the morning she'd arrived at his apartment and saved him from burning the place down. "Or some breakfast? I promise I'll do it better this time."

"Actually, I think we should talk."

His hand paused in midair as he reached to flip on the lights. Why didn't that sound positive? Her tone was as icy as a winter storm. He remembered the warmth of her kiss and decided kissing was definitely a better option. He had to get her relaxed. Then they'd talk. About their future.

"Later," he said, reaching for her, turning her toward him and wrapping his arms around her. He laced his fingers together at the base of her back. "Right now, I have a better idea."

"Brody—"

"Kiss me."

He didn't wait for her response. He captured her mouth. She acted as unresponsive as an unplugged computer. But he knew how she could respond. How she could lose abandon in his arms. He'd heard her moans of ecstasy. He'd felt her buck beneath him, crazed with desire.

She simply needed patience, reassurance, love. And he was ready and willing to offer all she needed.

When he angled his mouth across hers, her lips remained firm. But he refused to give up easily. Softly, temptingly, he tested the seam of her lips with his tongue, tickling, toying with her. She slammed her hands against his chest. He would have stopped then and set her away from him. Disappointment, confusion and anger blurring his rational thinking, he realized something had changed between them. And he had no idea what.

But before he could stop the kiss he'd mistakenly started, she curled her fingers into fists, tightened her grip on his shirt and pulled him closer. Slowly, she began to soften in his arms. It came in stages, bordering between resistance and eagerness. Her lips became pliable. Her body arched toward him.

When he realized he'd won, he picked her up, bracing her against his chest. While he continued kissing her, devouring her mouth with his, he moved through the dark den, past the windows where the drapes were drawn. The toes of her tennis shoes brushed against his shins. He felt her full breasts against him. And her arms slipped around his neck in surrender.

There was only one place for this to end—in bed.

He carried her full against him, her lower abdomen pressing against his erection, to the bedroom. When he reached the open door, he set her feet on the floor and bent to lift her into his arms.

"Oh, Brody," she said, breathless, "we need to talk."

"Not now, love. Not now." He bent to nuzzle her neck, to breathe in the warm scent of her skin.

"But—"

"What the hell do you think you're doing?" Another voice spoke in a harsh Australian accent.

Brody almost tripped over his own two feet.

Jillian gasped and jerked away from him.

Together, they looked toward the bed. In the deep shadows he could see the outline of a woman. With long hair. With dangerous curves. She reclined suggestively across his bed.

A jolt of recognition shot through him. He felt his insides collapse with shock. "Gail?"

"Yes, luv." She drawled the last word out in a sarcastic manner, mimicking him. "Like I said, what the hell are you doing? I've been waiting for you all damn night."

Tension tightened every muscle in his body, pulling them taut. "How did you get in here? What the hell are *you* doing?"

Gail swung to the side of the bed and stood out of the shadows. She wore only a black negligee and spiked heels. Her long fiery-red hair covered the tops of her breasts.

Numbness poured over Brody like ice water.

Jillian shook her head and took a step backward, bumping into Brody's chest. He bracketed her shoulders with his hands. But she shrugged off his touch, pushed away from him.

"I—I can't believe..." Her voice faltered. She stared at Gail. Then her gaze shifted to Brody. Accusing. Blaming. Condemning.

The sharp hatred in her blue-green eyes gutted him. His emotions poured out of him in a rush as he realized what she thought. Not again! Not this time. Not now that he'd tasted hope.

"Jillie…" He reached for her.

She slapped his hand away and backed toward the door.

"Don't even start. Don't try to explain." She put her hands to her ears and raced through his apartment for the front door.

"Jillie!" He chased after her. "Wait. You've got to hear me out. I didn't know—"

She swung on him. Her frigid gaze shot icicles at him. "I don't want to hear it. I believed you. I believed you when you said Gail lied before. But not now. Not after this."

"Jillie," he said in a stern, unrelenting voice, "I did not invite her here. I didn't know she was… waiting." He fought down the confusion to find the words to explain the unexplainable.

"How did she get in?" she asked, disbelief making her words crisp.

"I don't know. But I'm going to find out."

"No!" She backed toward the door.

He stalked toward her, desperate to prevent her from leaving. "Jillie, you can't leave. Not now. Not after—"

"Don't remind me of what we did." Shame brightened her cheeks. Shaking her head, she trembled. From rage or shock, he wasn't sure. "I don't want to think about it."

"We can't forget it. I can't forget it. Can you?"

"I made this mistake before." Her throat convulsed, the muscles straining as she gulped air. "But not again. Never again."

The catch in her voice skewered his heart. He was losing her. Losing her. And he couldn't find the words to stop her. Nothing made sense. None of this. "Jillie, please—"

Unshed tears made her eyes glisten. "You are a bigger fool than me," she said, venom injected into her voice, poisoning his heart, "for thinking you could get away with this."

Jerking open the door, she folded her arms over her stomach and escaped. He took one step after her, then felt a hand grip his shirt, yank him off balance.

"You can't go after her," Gail said, hanging on to him. "She's not worth it." She wrapped her arms and one of her legs around him, rubbing her body against him suggestively. "I've been waiting a long time for this. I'm not going to lose you to that woman."

"Get off of me," he growled. He struggled against her clinging arms. He left the apartment, dragging Gail as she clung to him in desperation. "I have to go get her. Jillie!"

"No!" Gail tugged on his arm. "You're mine."

He flung his arm wide, and she fell back a step. "I was never yours. Never."

She launched herself at him again, wrapping her arms around his neck from behind, her wrist pressing against his Adam's apple. He took several awkward steps forward, trying to reach Jillie. Frustrated, he rounded on Gail, pulling her off balance. "What the hell are you doing here, Gail?"

"I heard one of you Fortunes was getting married. I knew you'd come looking for *her*. I couldn't let you marry that woman from Texas. The one you thought you fell in love with at Winslow." She was clawing at him, her nails biting into his skin. "And I knew it. I knew you'd be here with her. That's why you came to Texas, isn't it?"

"What difference does it make to you?" He shrugged her off and sped down the hallway after Jillian.

By the time he reached the elevators, the doors were closing. He lunged for the narrowing opening, but it was too late. He caught a glimpse of tears coursing down Jillian's porcelain features. Dammit all to hell.

He ripped at the closed panels of the door. No use. He pressed the button, trying to get the doors to open. Nothing. No response. Frantic, he turned. He started toward the stairs, then he heard another elevator door slide open.

Darting inside, he punched the lighted button for the lobby. But the damn thing went up instead of down. His heart pounded. Each breath came hard and fast. Like an angry tiger, he felt caged, trapped. He stalked the inside of the elevator. Back and forth in front of the doors. Unable to escape. Unable to stop Jillian.

Minutes that seemed like hours later, he reached the lobby. He raced out the glass doorway leading to the circular drive. His gaze darted this way and that.

"Jillie?" he called.

"Mr. Fortune?" the valet inquired, stepping forward.

"The lady...the one with me...did she come this way? Did you see her leave?"

"Yes, sir. I hailed her a cab." He nodded toward

a yellow car, its taillights flashing red as it veered onto the main street in front of the high-rise.

Brody's world caved in on him, crushing the breath out of his lungs. He'd lost her. She'd never believe him now. Never.

Fourteen

"I've put in for a transfer." On Monday, Jillian stood in front of Brody's massive desk, her arms crossed over her stomach, trying to contain the nervous fluttering that felt more like the ravens from Hitchcock's *The Birds* rather than delicate butterflies.

"What?" He stared hard at her, his gray eyes stormy. "Jillie, if you'd just listen to me, we could—"

"It will probably take another couple of weeks," she explained, dismissing his attempt to make more excuses. He'd followed her to her sister's after she'd run out on him. She'd refused to let him in the house. She'd ignored his phone calls. And she'd come to a hard conclusion. This was the end. "Personnel will get you a replacement—"

"I don't want a replacement!" He slammed his hands on his desk out of frustration. "Why didn't you resign?" he asked.

"Because I need the medical benefits. I can't take the chance—" She stopped herself. It wasn't his concern.

"You couldn't take the chance that I would give you a poor recommendation?" he asked, his face growing red with anger. "Don't you know me better than that?"

"I don't know you at all." She'd done all the talk-ing, all the crying she planned to do. Now it was time to get on with her life. Once and for all. Without Brody.

She should have felt strong, secure in her decision, but she felt shaky, vulnerable. "If that's all—" she turned on her heel and headed toward the door "—then I'll get to work."

"No," he said, his voice curt with suppressed an-ger, "that's not all. I want to discuss this." He stood, shoving his chair behind him and leaning his full weight against the desk, his knuckles white against the dark wood.

"The folder you asked for is on the corner of your desk." With a trembling hand she twisted the brass knob.

He cursed, but she kept walking.

Without a backward glance, she settled in at her desk, ignoring the bagel he'd placed on the corner before she'd arrived that morning, and managing to focus on the spreadsheet she was preparing. A couple of hours passed without a word from Brody. But her gaze drifted often to that toasted bagel. Her tangled nerves wound tighter as she tried to deny his thought-fulness.

When noon arrived she retrieved her purse from the desk drawer and a sweater from the back of her chair and headed for the elevator. She wouldn't wait for Brody to order her lunch. She needed peace, quiet, the coolness of the fall weather. She'd grab a sand-wich at the corner deli and take a leisurely stroll through the downtown district, beneath a canopy of red, brown and orange foliage.

At first her steps were fast, clipped. Anxiety chased after her like a bull snorting and pawing the ground. But as the hour dwindled and her turkey on rye digested, her footsteps slowed to a leisurely pace, until she was almost dragging her feet before she had to return to the office, to face Brody.

She absorbed the sun's warmth as she concentrated on putting one foot ahead of the other. That was all she seemed capable of these days. If she focused on the moment at hand, on the immediate, she could survive each second, minute, hour, day. Then her thoughts couldn't drift toward Brody.

And she couldn't feel the anguish clawing at her. She wouldn't hear the voice in her head reminding her how stupid she'd been. Or the contradictory voice telling her Brody was the man for her.

When she settled back into the chair behind her desk, she situated the spreadsheet beside her computer and studied the figures for accuracy. The blinker on her phone buzzed.

"Yes, Mr. Fortune," she said in a strained, reserved tone. It took every ounce of restraint to remain calm, collected.

"I need to dictate a letter, Jillie." His nickname nettled her.

She gave a heavy sigh. Why couldn't he use the Dictaphone machine like everyone else? Irritated but unwilling to give him the satisfaction, she reached for her steno pad and pencil. Maybe he was testing her, trying to find a reason to let her go or to give her a bad recommendation.

Somehow that assessment didn't strike her as on target about Brody. Still, she wouldn't be careless, she'd be cautious. Avoiding his direct gaze as she walked into his office, she felt him watching her, studying her, observing her every move. Pushing a lock of hair behind her ear, she poised her pencil over the pad. Why had he continued to play innocent? Why did he *act* as if he wanted her when he had Gail to play with?

"How was lunch?" His warm, rugged voice drew her gaze to him like a bee to honey. He leaned back in his black leather chair, the sun from the windows along the far wall backlighting him. He templed his fingers beneath his square chin. His eyes looked like molten lava.

"To whom shall I address the letter?" she asked, her voice shaking.

He frowned at her avoidance of his question. "My brother, Griff. You remember him, don't you? You can send it to the Double Crown Ranch."

She wondered why he couldn't pick up the phone and call, but tilted her head, gave a crisp nod, and scribbled the name on the top of the paper. Then she paused, waiting for him to continue.

"Dear Griff," Brody dictated, swiveling his chair sideways until he faced away from her and stared out the windows.

His hawklike profile seemed remote, harsh, uncaring, as if he'd dismissed her as easily as someone shooed a fly buzzing around a bowl of soup. As easily as her father had discarded her from his life. A trembling rage shook her to the core.

"I have a situation that needs your attention," he stated, slowly, enunciating each word carefully.

Concentrating on each word, she blocked out the

pounding of her heart, the way it always beat chaotically when she heard him speak.

"Six months ago, when I was working in Sydney, I became acquainted with an old...friend of mine. Gail Harken, an investment banker with Jones, Blanchard, Seymour and Elliott..."

The pencil lead snapped off. Her stomach rolled. She glanced at Brody. Her pulse pounded in her ears. But he wasn't paying any attention to her. He simply continued speaking in a low monotone. Falling behind in the dictation, she grabbed for a spare pencil and tried to catch up, tried to ignore the roaring of her pulse in her ears.

"...and we were able to work together on several deals. It was a platonic relationship."

Jillian's shoulders stiffened. But she kept writing.

He grew silent, his eyes focusing on some distant spot out the window. Finally he said, "Uh, Jillie, where did I leave off?"

She frowned and read her shorthand. Grinding her teeth, she said, "'A platonic relationship.'"

"Ah, yes." He rubbed his hand over his jaw and she could almost feel the rasping along her nerve endings. "Recently," he said, "Gail surprised me..." He paused, scratched his temple. "Yeah, that's right. She surprised me with a visit here in the States. She had an offer, a new—" he cleared his throat "—proposal."

Jillian's pencil stilled, the lead digging a tiny hole into her pad.

"It came out of the blue," he said, "and threw a wrench into my plans." He glanced at her then. "Are you getting this?"

She nodded. But she wasn't taking shorthand anymore. Her hands shook too much.

Settling back into his chair, smugly looking away from her, he continued. "It was an offer I had to refuse. As it would have cost too much. And offered very few returns for my investment."

Her jaw clenched tight. She knew exactly what he was trying to do. And it wouldn't work. "Brody—"

He lifted a finger to stop her. "I don't want to lose this thought. I explained the situation to Gail. That my heart wasn't in the project." His gaze shifted toward Jillian. "I didn't want simple, short-term gains. My interest was occupied with something more permanent." He swung his chair around and faced Jillian again, the strength of his conviction leveling her with one look. "A lifetime investment."

She snapped her steno pad shut and rose on wobbly legs. "This won't work. If you have serious work for me to do, I'll be at my desk."

For long moments after Jillian left his office, Brody tapped a pen against the hard surface of his desk. He couldn't hear the erratic tapping, only the pounding of his heart.

You've lost her. Lost her for good.

As if something heavy and restrictive weighted him down, he felt unable to move, unable to even blink. He stared at the door leading to Jillian's desk. To her. But he didn't really see the solid oak door. He only saw the barrier keeping him out of her heart.

He'd lost. Unable to even defend himself. She'd blocked him out. His explanations fell on deaf ears.

It's fate. He'd believed that before, when she'd left

Winslow suddenly, when he'd received her letter that she'd married James, when he'd come to Texas and found her in his very own office. And now fate was taking her away from him. Again.

But was it that simple? Could he accept that as an explanation and move on? Without Jillian? Maybe it was fate. But was it working for or against him this time? Maybe the odds had been stacked against them from the beginning. But that didn't have to mean they couldn't be together. Unsure, he felt an iron band tighten across the back of his neck.

Until he reached Jillian, until he fought as hard and as long as he could fight, he would be her prisoner, bound to her by a love so strong. He felt the inflexible cords wrapped around his heart.

He couldn't give up. Not this time.

Not after the passion they'd shared. Not when he burned for her. And yearned for more.

I love her. That was a fact. No longer just a feeling burrowed inside his heart. His soul radiated that truth with every breath.

He believed some part of her, even if it was minuscule, loved him, or had loved him, too. Or else she wouldn't have made love with him. She wouldn't have cared so much about Gail. Or about his perceived betrayal. She loved him. He just had to make her realize she couldn't live without him. He had to show her she could trust him.

At precisely five o'clock, as if she'd been watching and waiting for the clock to reach that time all day, his intercom buzzed. "If you don't have any more work for me this afternoon, Mr. Fortune," she said, "I'll be leaving for the day."

His hands clenched each time she used that formality. "There is something I need," he said back to her, through the crackling speaker. "Could you step into my office?"

A pause pulsed between them, filling his ears with static, before she responded. "Of course."

When she stepped inside his office, he shut the door behind her. She turned around fast, her eyes wide.

"Brody—" Her voice took on an uncompromising edge.

Without regrets, he locked the bolt and put the key in his pocket. "We have something to discuss."

She crossed her arms over her chest. "Brody, I don't have time for this. I have—"

"Tough." He nodded toward the chair in front of his desk. He walked past her and slung a hip onto the corner. He glared at her. "Sit down. You're going to hear me out. Then if you still want to walk out that door, fine. I won't stop you."

With an irritated sigh, she moved stiffly to the chair and sat on the edge of the cushioned seat. The prim line of her shoulders looked unrelenting. She clasped her hands tightly in her lap. Her mouth was drawn into a thin, straight line. God, he could remember how sweet and tempting she tasted. He knew it would take one hell of an explanation to convince her now.

But he had to succeed.

"Jillie, the other night, I was as surprised as you were by Gail's arrival. I didn't know she was coming here. I hadn't been in contact with her for months. And then it had only been in a professional way."

"The way our professional relationship ended up in the bedroom."

He flinched inwardly but maintained his negotiator's mask. "No. I never slept with Gail. In college. Or after. She wanted to, I won't deny that, but I'm not responsible for her actions. Only my own."

She grabbed the arms of the chair as if to rise. "I don't want to hear this."

"Too damn bad. You're going to." He leaned forward, bracing his hand on his knee. "You're going to hear every damn word of it."

With a huff of indignation, she scooted back into the safety of the chair and crossed her arms over her growing stomach. "Fine, get on with it. I have an appointment in an hour that I can't miss."

"A doctor's appointment?" he asked, concern tightening his shoulders.

"It's really none of your concern. Is it?"

"Jillie—" He reached out to her, but let his hand fall back to his thigh. "I love you. I care about you. About the baby."

She tilted her head and glared at him. "What were you saying?"

He sucked in a shaky breath. He'd laid his feelings on the table. And she didn't care. She didn't give a damn. Yet an urgency inside him wouldn't let him quit. He'd never been a quitter. Never. Either in academics, sports, or in business. This time, he'd handle love the way he handled business acquisitions—with bankable determination. "I figured out how Gail got into my apartment. Are you mildly curious about how she got there?"

"I assume with a key." Her voice betrayed nothing. "Yours?"

"The manager's," he countered.

She blinked slowly, as if digesting that news. But her features registered disbelief. "Right."

"If you want, I'll have the manager confess his sins, his weakness to a pretty woman with a sorry line. Whatever it takes for you to believe me."

"That won't be necessary. Gail isn't my concern."

"What is?"

She glanced away from him. She looked pale. Tiny blue circles smudged the delicate skin beneath her eyes. He could see through her anger now to the depth of pain that reflected his own.

"Jillie, what is it? If not Gail, then what?"

She leveled him with those startling blue-green eyes. "You."

"I know you don't trust me. But if you'll just hear me out, I think you'll finally understand that it was all a mistake. Gail—"

"I told you," she snapped. "Gail isn't the issue. Maybe she was the last straw."

"Then, what is it?"

"It's not just what you did. Or didn't do." She conceded his point that he might be telling the truth. That gave him a smidgen of hope. "It's what you said...that night."

"What? Tell me. Maybe you misunderstood me."

She shook her head. Her throat convulsed. "You were right. I'm not good enough for you. I never have been."

"What? I never said that."

"Not directly. But you implied it when you wished you'd been my first lover. That this child of mine was yours. Not James's." She flung his words back into his face, her voice shaking.

"Jillie, that's not what I meant." But his heart tripped over itself. Or was that exactly what he'd meant? Had she hit the core of his reluctance, his doubts, his fears?

"Oh? Then, what is it? Explain it to me. Tell me you want this child as much as I do." She stood, challenging him, daring him to deny it. "Tell me you love me and all that goes with that—my baby. That you can raise it as your own. Without regrets."

Brody stood. Trying to gather his thoughts, he traced the length of his desk, pacing back and forth, trying to explain away what she'd said. But his own fears pulsed through him. She was right. He had doubts. Lots of them.

Finally he faced her. His throat burned. "I don't have an answer for you. Not yet." But there had to be a solution. Maybe he just needed time. Maybe they needed time together. "Don't be so hasty. Give us time. We can sort through this."

"Sort through it? Sort through it?" Her voice quaked with unleashed emotions. "This isn't a merger. This isn't negotiable. There's nothing to sort through. Either you love us or you don't. And from the hesitancy in your eyes, I see time's up." She trembled, shaking with rage, her face mottling with anger.

Denials filed inside his head. Reasons lined up. But words stuck in his throat.

"I don't have time to make any more stupid mistakes in my life. No more chances. Not when I have this little life depending on me." Her hand touched her slightly rounded abdomen. Tears glistened in her eyes. "It's over, Brody. Over for good. I should have let go of any feelings I had for you ten years ago. But I didn't. I hung on to them, nurtured them. But no more. This is it.

"Now, will you unlock the door and let me leave?" She glared at him, daring him to refuse.

His heart thudded dully in his chest, as if every ounce of feeling had been drained out of him. Shock sunk into his bones, paralyzing him. He gave a slow nod. He had nothing left to say. She'd won.

But what had they both lost?

Brody had no energy. He felt nothing. He had no appetite. No desire. No need or wants. Except Jillian. And that was an impossibility.

He sat on the supple leather sofa in Ryan Fortune's study. He looked out the window at the courtyard, staring at the few leaves scattered along the tiled pathways but not seeing anything at all. Only Jillian's face emerged in his mind, tight with suppressed emotions, resentment and anger churning in her blue-green eyes.

He remembered dancing with her in this very courtyard only a week ago. Her hand tucked securely in his, her chin tilted toward him. Hope, longing, desire pulling them together. They had been unable to resist.

Now it was gone, as faded and discarded as the flowers from the wedding that had drooped and fallen only to be swept away with brooms and dustpans. A brisk wind blew through the courtyard, and Brody could feel it deep in his bones, as if Jillian's confrontation had left a wind tunnel through his empty, bereft soul.

He didn't know how long he'd been sitting there. He could barely remember driving to the Double

Crown Ranch late last night after Jillian had left him standing in his office. He'd remained there a long time, feeling the loneliness settle around him like a heavy, suffocating cloak. He'd reached the ranch well after dinner had been served and had barely nodded a greeting to the other Fortunes. He'd trudged up the stairs to the room he'd used when he'd visited the ranch on weekends and fallen onto the bed.

But he hadn't slept. He couldn't.

He'd been right when he'd told Jillian when someone was hurting, aching, miserable, they needed their family, a home, a safe haven. But being among loved ones didn't make Brody feel much better. Anger and sadness warred inside him, crippling him until he couldn't think, move or respond.

Unable to lie in bed any longer, he'd risen before dawn, showered and found his way to Uncle Ryan's study. From the slant of the sunlight, he'd been sitting here for hours. Or maybe it just seemed that long when someone rapped on the door.

"Yes?" he rasped, his throat raw, his voice hoarse.

The door creaked as it opened, and his father peered inside, his tanned, leathery brow wrinkled into a frown. "Here you are, Son."

"Do you need the study? Does Uncle Ryan?"

Tall and wiry, Teddy Fortune entered the high-beamed room. "No, you're fine. Mind if I come in?"

"Go ahead." Brody slanted his gaze toward the stone fireplace. An unfinished beam created the mantel. He stared at the blackened grate and felt the ashes of doubts and regrets pile up in his soul.

Teddy sank into the chair beside Brody. He laid his large hands over the rounded arms of the chair, his fingers curling over the edges. He tapped the leather with his wedding ring. "Trouble at work?" he asked. "With the merger?"

"No, sir. It's going smoothly. Everything is ready for the board meeting tomorrow." Then what? he wondered. Would he return to Australia? Would he stay here in San Antonio? He couldn't imagine doing anything without Jillie.

"Good. Good." His father nodded his approval.

Brody heard the ticking of the intricately carved Spanish clock over the mantel and his father's deep, resonating breaths.

"Anything else bothering you?" Teddy asked.

"Nope."

"I see." Teddy chuckled and crossed his arms over his chest. "Women trouble, eh?"

Brody cut his eyes toward his father. "I don't want to talk about it."

"Okay." Teddy looked at the fireplace. "We heard from the honeymooners last night."

"Reed and Mallory?"

Teddy nodded. "Yeah. They're doing fine. Enjoying themselves, I'd say."

"Who wouldn't on a deserted stretch of beach with a beautiful woman?" His remark sounded caustic even to himself and he regretted the statement.

"You're not jealous of your brother, are you, Son?"

"No, sir." And he wasn't. It had been obvious how much Reed and Mallory loved each other. He simply wanted what they had. And he'd thought he'd found it with Jillie. How had everything gone so wrong?

He knew the answer. It was his fault. His selfishness, his foolishness, his muddled thinking had come between him and the woman he loved.

"I didn't think so." Teddy shifted in his seat, making the leather creak, and crossed one booted foot over his other knee. "So what is it, then?"

"Dad, I'm not thirteen. I can handle this myself."

"Good. I didn't raise you boys to come running home to daddy every time something goes wrong. I see I did my job well."

Brody felt a tug on the corner of his mouth.

"We'll just sit here together. In the quiet. We don't have to talk. We can just commune with the…fireplace there."

Brody fought the urge to smile at his father's caginess. Several minutes passed without either one saying a word. Teddy Fortune had proven his patience with horses years before. And now he used that same patience with his son. He knew his father would sit there waiting for an eternity until Brody explained his problem. How could simple words convey what had gone so terribly wrong?

"You're right, Dad."

"About?" Teddy asked, his voice gentle with years of wisdom.

"It's about a woman."

"Usually is, Son. Just 'cause I've been married a long time doesn't mean the trouble stops once you say 'I do.'"

A tightness seized Brody's chest. "Well, I won't be saying, 'I do.'"

"That so?"

He nodded. "Not that I'm not willing."

Or was he? Like tiny, sharp thorns, doubts pressed

into his thoughts once more. Could he really, honestly say he was willing to marry Jillian? He knew what was stopping him. And there wasn't any way to overcome it.

"The lady's not so inclined, eh?"

"That's right." Or at least that was part of it. A small part. "I suppose I'm not, either. Maybe I'm commitment-phobic. Maybe she's not the right one." He tried voicing some of his questions, but they rang with a false note.

Brody leaned forward and shot his fingers through his hair, clawing at his skull. If only he could rip those questions out of his head. If only he could get rid of the doubts. But he couldn't. They were there. And he had to acknowledge them. "I don't know what the hell is wrong with me."

"You don't look like a man who's thrilled that he's off that matrimonial hook."

"I'm not. But I guess there's no way I can marry her, either."

"It does take two willing adults."

Brody shook his head. "The real trouble isn't her. It's me."

Teddy nodded as if he understood. Brody wished to hell he did.

"I've got these damn questions that won't turn me loose. They won't let me make that commitment. I thought I was ready. I thought I loved her enough. But, hell, maybe I don't."

"Well, if misery is any evidence of love then I'd say you've got it pretty darn bad. So what is it that's holding you back?"

He released a deep heavy sigh, full of all his anguish and regrets. "She's pregnant."

"By you?"

"No. If I was the father, then it would be easy. So easy. I'd marry her in a heartbeat."

"I see." Teddy scratched his jaw.

Brody looked at his father then. "You do?"

"Sure. You don't know if you'll love this kid. If you can raise it as your own. It's perfectly understandable."

"It is?"

Sagely, Teddy nodded. "Don't worry about it, Son. It's for the best. At least you realized this now...rather than after you'd married the woman. Nope, this is definitely for the best. No use marrying a woman who's pregnant with another man's baby. Raising another man's child will only lead to trouble."

Brody raised his eyebrows. This didn't sound like his father. Maybe he hadn't explained the situation fully. "She's not a loose woman. She doesn't fool around. She was married and her husband—"

"The reasons don't matter, Son. Your feelings do. Better you realized it now. Just walk away. Free and clear."

His insides twisted. "I don't feel free. I feel like a damn coward. I've never backed away from adversity before. Why now?"

Teddy put his hand on Brody's shoulder, his grip strong and firm. "Because marriage is forever. Raising a kid, hell, that's permanent. You can't risk losing on that score."

"You don't think it sounds pathetic?"

"Nah, it's understandable. I'd feel the same way."

Stunned by his father's statement, Brody said, "You would?"

"Sure. When Griff showed up as a little boy on our property, I had plenty of doubts. Lots of questions. I didn't know where this kid came from. What he'd been through. It was obvious he'd been treated roughly. I could have been bringing trouble right to our back door."

Brody nodded, agreeing with his father, understanding his father as an adult. "I've thought about that. About how Griff has always kept himself a little distant from the family. Made me think about…you know, Jillie's baby. How it would accept me as its daddy."

"Thinking is good. I worried over Griff many a night. Hell, I already had a family, already had you kids. I didn't need any more. Your mother had her hands full chasing you all around. Why burden her more? Why should I risk all we had for this stray?

"And I remembered being raised by my grandpa. Never knew a meaner son of a gun. I was a pawn to him. Not a son. Just something to get back at my father with. And I got mad for the first time in years."

"So what changed your mind about adopting Griff?" A cold sweat dampened Brody's forehead.

"Your mother," Teddy said simply, eloquently. "She believed Griff only needed someone to show him a little love, a little kindness. And I'd say she was right. He turned out fine. Better than that. I'm damn proud to call him my son."

Brody's thoughts churned.

"And so will you be about this kid," Teddy said, surprising Brody even more.

Brody cut his eyes toward his father. Love and understanding shone in those deep-set gray eyes, mirroring Brody's.

"This kid won't know anyone else as his father," Teddy said. "It's not the same situation at all. This baby will love you. And you'll love him. You'll see."

His doubts seemed suddenly smaller, more trivial than before. Hope sprang inside him. He wanted to latch on to his father's words and believe them. But could he? Would that see him through the next twenty years? "You think so?"

"I know so. I can see you love this woman something awful. That love will transmit itself to her child...your child. You'll love the little rascal more than you can imagine right now."

Brody remained silent, digesting all his father had said. His heart ached with the prospect of losing Jillian. Or had he lost her already? That fear galvanized him. He loved her more than anything or anyone he'd ever known. He needed her, more than he needed his family. He knew that if he lost her, his life would be worthless. If he didn't help her raise her baby, then he'd be missing out on more than he could imagine. His heart ached with a raw emptiness that only Jillie and her baby could fill.

"So, I'm going to be a grandpa." Teddy chuckled and clapped Brody on the back. "Think we better get the wedding plans under way."

Brody felt a cold chill through to his bones. "I think the lady has a few objections."

"Then, Son, you better figure out a way to fix things and win the lady's heart."

Brody knew then that his father was right. His situation still seemed dark as midnight, but he could now see a distant light of hope filter through the darkness. He could finally see things from a different angle. Thanks to his father's help.

His shoulders squared. He wasn't a damn coward. Because he wasn't giving up on Jillian or their love. He might need every ounce of love to convince her that she needed him, too. And that she could trust him. But no matter what, he wasn't giving up this time.

Fifteen

Something was wrong. Terribly wrong. Jillian should have felt relief. After all, this was the day of the big board meeting. Her job with Brody would soon be finished. Only a few more hours and she wouldn't have to see him again. She'd already decided to take a vacation until Personnel could transfer her. So why did she feel shaky, panicky?

And why was Brody suddenly ignoring her, no longer trying to discuss their relationship? He didn't act angry or sad. In fact, he seemed downright chipper. There was a bounce in his step. An easy smile on his face. She was the one rebounding between rage and an incredible sadness that seemed to wash over her with the force of a hurricane.

What had happened? Had he finally accepted that nothing could ever be between them? Anger bubbled up inside her. Wasn't that what she wanted? Her insides twisted sharply with doubt.

How had he turned off his emotions as if he'd switched off a light? Frustration boiled inside her. Why couldn't she turn off those same heart-wrenching, tumultuous emotions? Why did she feel like ranting one minute and crying the next?

As the day wore on, the hours slipping through her fingers like sand in an hourglass, the board meeting approached, as did the moment when she would finally tell Brody goodbye. Every muscle in her body constricted. Her jaw clenched tighter and tighter, as if the hinges were being screwed shut. She made more mistakes. Her hands trembled, her fingers unable to find the right keys on the keyboard or calculator. Her thoughts centered on Brody, her mind unable to focus on any task.

And Brody had the patience of a saint. She wanted to slap him. Or her. She wasn't sure which.

"How's it going?" Amy asked when she called that afternoon.

"Not much longer." Even the words were hard to say. Her heart felt incapable of giving a full, complete beat. "The board meeting is in a few minutes. Brody's already in the boardroom, so I can't talk long."

"You'll feel better when this is all behind you." Her sister's encouraging, supportive voice didn't give Jillian much hope.

She shrugged and hooked the phone between her chin and shoulder. "I hope so."

"Perk up! This is what you wanted, isn't it?"

"Maybe…yes…no. I don't know." Her voice resonated with questions and doubts.

"Did you tell Brody that you were taking a vacation starting tomorrow?" Amy asked.

"That's just it. He didn't seem perturbed in the least. He simply said that was fine." Her throat burned. His indifference had yanked her up short. "Said he wouldn't need my help after the board meeting anyway."

"Good. I'm glad he didn't give you any flak."

Amy paused, then asked, "How come you don't sound relieved?"

Raking her hair back out of her face, Jillian felt a cold sweat break out along her spine. "I don't know. It's like Brody has forgotten I exist."

"Isn't that what you wanted?"

"Stop saying that!" She sighed heavily. Her shoulders slumped with fatigue. "I guess. But now that he has... I didn't realize how much it would hurt."

"Or how much you loved him," Amy supplied.

Jillian shook her head. "No. I've known that a long time. But I thought it would be easier somehow."

"And it's not."

"It makes me mad. Mad at him. Mad at me." Her hands clenched. "What a fool I was to believe he could care for me!" She fell back against her chair. "This just proves I was right. He didn't love me...or the baby. He didn't care enough." Her voice cracked. "I made the right decision. Finally." She sighed wearily. "What a mess I've made of my life."

"Nonsense." Amy refuted her statement. "You know something, Sis? I've never told you this before, but I admire you." At Jillian's doubtful laugh, she added, "It's true!

"Even though you were married to a lousy man, you tried to make it work. You didn't want James to die. You certainly didn't want to end up an unwed mother with a mountain of debt. But you've handled it with class, without complaints. You've worked every step of the way to make your life, and the life for your baby, better."

The first smile in a week touched Jillian's taut mouth. "When did you get so bossy?"

"Just trying to protect my little sister."

"Well, nothing will protect me this afternoon. All the legal documents will be signed. All the *t*'s crossed. The *i*'s dotted. The merger will be complete."

Amy remained silent for a few seconds before asking, "Will Brody be heading back to Australia?"

Just the thought of him being thousands of miles away made her insides throb. "I don't know. But I would imagine. There's nothing to keep him here."

Maybe out of sight meant he'd be out of her heart, too. But she knew better. It had never been the case with Brody Fortune. "And that," she said, feeling her heart ripping into tiny shreds, "will be the end of that."

Jillian's eyes burned. She felt like a zombie sitting in the opulent setting of the boardroom. Activity swirled around her. She tried to sort through the spreadsheets, but the numbers blurred. This is the room where she'd first seen Brody again. And had fainted right into his arms.

At the memory of that first kiss and reunion, a heat radiated from her heart, fried her insides until she felt herself shriveling, crumpling. She shoved aside those thoughts and concentrated on setting up the overhead projector and placing copies of the legal document containing the specifications of the merger around the long oval table.

Over the next twenty minutes, the Fortunes, from the dignified Ryan Fortune and his offspring to his rugged, long-lost brother Teddy and his family, filed into the room, their voices blending and merging into a low rumble of excitement. Each of the children had been called in to sign the documents that would make the merger complete. She recognized most from meeting them at the recent wedding.

Before the meeting started, Brody took her aside. Dressed in his expensive suit and red tie, he looked powerful, in command. But she recognized the telltale tick in his temple that broadcast his anxiety. She wondered if he realized this was it. After the meeting they'd no longer see each other. There was no going back. This time their goodbye would be forever.

Her stomach lurched, her heart pounding weakly without a sure rhythm, without strength. They'd said it all. If she only knew that he loved her, then she would fight for their future. But the sad truth slapped her in the face. He didn't care.

All he cared about was this merger.

Oblivious to the turmoil inside her, he asked in his brusque accent, "Can you get my briefcase from my office?"

"Sure," she said, eager for a few minutes alone to try to contain her anger, her paralyzing sadness.

Wanting to reassure him that he was prepared, or maybe she simply needed her own reassurance, she said in a hushed whisper, "Don't worry. Everything is all right."

He gave her a tight smile. "I hope you're right. This…merger means everything to me."

Her heart caved in, and she blinked back acidic tears.

"But it's going to take—" he glanced around the room "—cooperation from everyone. I can't do it without you."

His statement stumped her. She hadn't heard rumors of disgruntled family members. It seemed to be a prosperous deal for all concerned. Maybe he feared some jealous sibling would balk.

When she returned to the boardroom with Brody's briefcase, the smooth leather the same deep, rich shade as the gleaming, polished table, everyone had settled into their places around the table. Brody stood at the far end and cleared his throat. As he began to explain the legalities of the merger to his family, he readjusted his tie as if it were strangling him. Only she seemed to notice his nervousness. She figured he wanted to impress his father and uncle.

A light rap on the door interrupted Brody's prepared speech. His head snapped up, and he paused in his explanation of why he'd been chosen to handle the merger.

"Jillie," he said in that voice that made her toes curl, "would you see who that is?"

She gave a nod and pushed away from the table. Opening the paneled wooden door, she felt a gasp lodge in her throat. Her heart came to a complete stop as she stared right at Gail.

Dressed in a black suit, she looked cosmopolitan, making Jillian feel dumpy and unattractive. Gail's heavily painted red lips spread into a cool smile. "Sorry I'm late." She sailed past Jillian as if she was supposed to be here and settled herself into Jillian's vacant chair, successfully occupying the last seat. "G'day, all."

Jillian's heart gave a faint flutter, increasing with each second, beating harder and faster until anger pumped through her veins. Her face flushed. Her ears roared.

"Thank you for coming," Brody said. His mouth quirked into a secretive smile as he looked back at his notes.

Jillian's world tilted crazily out of sync. What was happening? Why was Gail here? The realization that they'd been working together on this project, without Jillian's knowledge, and probably doing a lot of other things made Jillian's knees weak and wobbly. It took every ounce of determination to remain standing.

"Now that we're all here," Brody said, his voice firm and solid.

He didn't even seem concerned that Jillian had no place to sit. She stood on the sidelines...once again. She felt as conspicuous as intimate apparel flapping in the breeze on an old-fashioned drying line. Anger fired her temper like a bottle rocket.

"We can get started." Brody looked toward her, then. "Jillian, if you could put up the first overhead."

Her hands clenched into fists. She wanted to walk right out the door and never look back. She opened her mouth to tell Brody off once and for all. Then snapped it shut. What was she going to do? Make a scene in front of the board? Get herself fired? No way. Brody was wrapping up this deal, then he was probably going back to Sydney. With Gail. What did she care if he slept with a barracuda? What did she care...?

She almost collapsed with despair, and the love she'd felt for Brody weighed heavily on her. She wouldn't—couldn't think about that now. She had to finish this meeting. Then she could leave. She could mourn for however long it took to get Brody out of her system. Until then, she needed to keep this job. She wouldn't let him get the best of her. Not this time.

A numbness winding through her, she walked stiff-kneed over to the projector. Maybe that's why he'd been in such a wonderful mood today. Maybe he and Gail had reunited after their last argument, after Jillian had shown him his fears and why their relationship couldn't work. Maybe that's why he hadn't seemed to need or care about her anymore. Hot, angry tears seared her eyes.

Switching on the projector, her hands shaking so badly she thought someone had to notice, she determined to survive this meeting. Later she could collapse. She could cry until she had no more tears. But then she would forget Brody Fortune as easily as he'd forgotten her.

She glanced at the wall to be sure the projection was focused on the screen. Confusion clouded her mind. Her heart stopped. Her hands turned to ice.

What was this? A hand-written note had been placed on the overhead. She recognized Brody's penmanship. The bold lines. The cautious slant. She reached to remove it and replace it with the correct one. Then her hand faltered. She read it again. Slowly this time.

Jillian, will you marry me? I love you. I've always loved you. Brody.

Time telescoped into what seemed like a time warp, as if the world had suddenly slowed. Her movements seemed heavy and awkward. Her breathing laborious. But her heart almost bolted out of her chest.

"Before we settle the merger," Brody said, his

voice sounding strained, "we have another family matter to handle. A different kind of a merger."

She felt all eyes in the room focus on her. Especially Brody's. His eyes were warm, friendly, imploring, and turned her emotions inside out. Her mind spun out of control. She could barely hear his words over the pounding of her heart.

Suddenly his words before the meeting— *This...merger means everything to me*—made sense. Her nerves unraveled like a ball of twine. She shook so hard that she figured the floor beneath her had to be causing it. But the tremors came from deep inside her.

"Jillie," he said, his voice infinitely calmer than her erratic pulse, "it seems as if circumstances have always been against us. But not today. This time, I'm going to set the record straight. And if you don't believe me, then you'll have to listen to these testimonies."

"What are you doing?" she asked, her voice barely above a whisper. "Why are you doing this?" She could only mouth the question as turbulent emotions clogged her throat. Was he making fun of her? Trying to humiliate her?

Then Teddy Fortune spoke. "Lady," he said, leveling her with steely gray eyes that reminded her of Brody, "you've tangled my son in knots. I've never seen him so miserable." His voice resonated with raw emotion that only a parent feels for his child. He pulled a red rose from beneath the table and laid it in the center. "He is one hundred percent in love with you."

"I can testify to that," Griff said, adding a rose to

their father's. "And I can tell you that he's never been serious with a woman. Before or since he first met you. You're the only one for him."

"Well, I suppose it's my turn," Gail said, her features drawn tight. She plunked down another rose. Her nail polish matched the deep, red hue. "I put up a damn good fight, but it looks like you won.

"Anybody who knows me, knows that I never admit defeat. But I suppose I have to now." Her gaze shifted toward Brody. "That, or Brody would cancel every deal we've ever made, no matter the price he paid or money he could lose.

"So—" she gave a shoulder-shrugging sigh "—I'm here to tell you that he definitely loves you. Not me. I sensed I was about to lose back at Winslow. That's why I told you...that tiny white lie."

"Gail," Brody interrupted.

"Okay." She gave a huff of indignation or maybe annoyance as she tapped a silver-plated pen against the table. "It was a bald-faced lie. And that's why I flew over here to the States. To stop him from marrying you. But it's obvious even to me that he could never be interested in anything with me. Not since you entered his life."

With each person's confession and testimony, Jillian's heartbeat crescendoed to a deafening roar. Her limbs began to quake. And her gaze remained locked with Brody's. The love and warmth she saw in his eyes began to melt the icy edges of her heart.

Around the table they went, one after the other, placing more roses on the growing bouquet in the center. Each testified to Brody's love for Jillian and his miserable state since she broke up with him.

Finally, Brody moved toward her, his steps slow and decisive. He pulled a black velvet ring box out of his coat pocket and propped open the lid. A diamond that would have definitely been Marilyn Monroe's best friend winked and twinkled in the light. But Jillian had never wanted Brody's riches. She'd never wanted a fancy house, expensive cars, or jewels fit for a princess.

She only wanted a home. With a man to love. And a man to love her.

When he stood directly in front of her, he spoke. "I love you, Jillie." His voice was thick with emotion. His taut skin stretched as his Adam's apple plunged and bobbed with a hard swallow. "I know it's hard for you to believe. That's why I had to bring my family here today. To try to convince you that I can't go on without you."

He cleared his throat again, shifted from foot to foot. "I understand your fears, your hesitations. I know I haven't given you a lot of reasons to love me in return. But I ask you for one more chance."

Then he dropped to one knee in front of her.

She felt her own throat contract with the surge of tears. He took her hand in his, smoothing his thumb over her ring finger, sending sparks of awareness down her spine and tenderness welling in her heart.

"I want to marry you, Jillie. I think I've wanted you since the day we met. Do you remember that day? I do," he said without waiting for her to respond. "It was September twenty-fourth. I remember how warm it was that day. How brilliant the sky looked. How beautiful you were. Still are." He gave her a smile that could have melted an iceberg. "I came to Texas to find you."

"That's true," Griff interjected. "He told me about you six months ago. He wanted me to try and locate—"

"But you were already here. Waiting for me. Seeing you again was like a miracle. I want to spend every day of my life trying to make you as happy as you made me that first day we met. I want to help you bring this baby into the world, love him or her, cherish you both and help the baby grow up to be someone as kind and wonderful as you, Jillie."

She wasn't sure how she could be standing. She felt her whole body trembling. She clung to his hand for balance. Was this real, she wondered, or a dream?

"But you were right," Brody continued, "when you said I had doubts and questions about raising this baby."

Her heart dipped low into her belly and she felt the sick feeling she'd felt the morning after they'd made love.

"I don't deny that. But you have to know that the idea of raising this child with you scares the hell out of me. The responsibility is awesome. But you know I don't run away from anything. Especially not you. I can't imagine a better way to spend my life, than loving you...and this child.

"But to prove to you that I'm not just making an empty promise... In this merger, there is a clause that not only ensures all of Ryan's and Teddy's grandchildren will have their own places on the board some day and their own shares of Fortune stock, but you and the baby have been included, as well."

The chill she'd felt all morning began to ease and her shuddering grew faint. "That's not what I wanted. I don't care about the money. I only wanted you."

"I know that. But I need you to know that I'm not like James. I want to make sure you are taken care of, that you have all you ever need. You don't ever have to worry about our baby."

Our baby. Her heart skipped a full beat. Was she hearing him correctly? Had his heart changed?

"This baby will be ours. We'll raise it together. And he or she will have the family you never had. A home. Our baby will be a Fortune."

With unshed tears glittering in his eyes, he said, "Jillie," his tongue rolling over her name and erasing her doubts and questions, "will you marry me?"

She bent and kissed him, her hand cupping his strong, fierce jaw, her mouth locking with his, fusing with his in a solemn vow.

"I'd say that was a yes." Teddy Fortune gave a hearty laugh.

The rest of the family clapped and cheered. Jillian didn't bother to see Gail's reaction. She no longer cared about that woman. Gail no longer held any power over Jillian. She no longer felt unworthy, but cherished. By Brody. And his family. She only cared for this man...and the life they'd make together.

Brody stood and pulled her into his solid embrace. "I need to hear you say it."

She ran her thumb along the sexy curve of his bottom lip. "Brody, I've loved you for a long, long time. And I'm going to keep right on loving you. Forever. Yes, I'll marry you."

He slanted his mouth over hers, bending her back

over his arm, and kissed her until she couldn't think, but could only feel the incredible love binding them together. Between them, nestled inside her, was their baby. And the beginning of their new life...together.

"Looks like there's gonna be another wedding in the family," Ryan Fortune said.

* * * * *

LEGACIES . LIES . LOVE .

*The glamour and mystery of this
fascinating NEW 12-book series
continues in November 2003...*

RING OF DECEPTION

by favorite Harlequin Presents® author

Sandra Marton

Detective Luke Sloan was hard-edged, intimidating...
and completely out of his element working
undercover in the Forrester Square Day Care!
He was suspicious of single mom Abby Douglas...
but when he realized that her fear was over something—
or *someone*—far more dangerous than himself,
the man in him needed to protect her.

*Forrester Square...
Legacies. Lies. Love.*

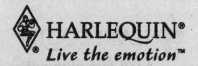

HARLEQUIN®
Live the emotion™

Visit us at www.forrestersquare.com

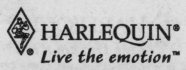

**From Silhouette Books comes
an exciting NEW spin-off to *The Coltons!***

PROTECTING
PEGGY

by award-winning author
Maggie Price

When FBI forensic scientist
Rory Sinclair checks into
Peggy Honeywell's inn late
one night, the sexy bachelor
finds himself smitten with the
single mother. While Rory works
undercover to solve the mystery
at a nearby children's ranch, his
feelings for Peggy grow…but
will his deception shake the
fragile foundation of their
newfound love?

Coming in December 2003.

THE COLTONS
FAMILY. PRIVILEGE. POWER.

Silhouette®

Where love comes alive™

Stories of shocking truths revealed!

PRIVATE SCANDALS

A brand-new collection from

JOANNA WAYNE
JUDY CHRISTENBERRY
TORI CARRINGTON

From three of the romance genre's most enthralling authors comes this trio of novellas about secret agendas, deep passions and hidden pasts. But not all scandals can be kept private!

Coming in January 2004.

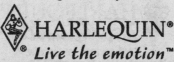

Forrester Square

LEGACIES. LIES. LOVE.

*Award-winning author Day Leclaire
brings a highly emotional and
exciting reunion romance story to
Forrester Square in December...*

KEEPING FAITH
by
Day Leclaire

Faith Marshall's dream of a "white-picket" life with
Ethan Dunn disappeared—along with her husband—
when she discovered that he was really a dangerous
mercenary. With Ethan missing in action, Faith found
herself alone, pregnant and struggling to survive.
Now, years later, Ethan turns up alive. Will a family
reunion be possible after so much deception?

*Forrester Square...
Legacies. Lies. Love.*

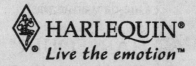

Live the emotion™